So, right there, just like he remembered. God, it had been so long, but it seemed like yesterday, shining in his memory.

He bit a little, letting it sting enough that Trey flailed and grabbed for him.

"I got you, honey," he murmured. "You're just fine."

"That burned so good."

"Did it? Can try it again." He grinned, slow and easy, just ready to try all the things.

"Please." Trey lifted his chin.

So Ap bit down, worrying that spot with his teeth. He never spent time playing, experimenting. Marking. This was a damn fun way to spend an evening.

WELCOME TO

Dear Reader,

Love is the dream. It dazzles us, makes us stronger, and brings us to our knees. Dreamspun Desires tell stories of love featuring your favorite heartwarming heroes, captivating plots, and exotic locations. Stories that make your breath catch and your imagination soar.

In the pages of these wonderful love stories, readers can escape to a world where love conquers all, the tenderness of a first kiss sweeps you away, and your heart pounds at the sight of the one you love.

When you put it all together, you find romance in its truest form.

Love always finds a way.

Elizabeth North

Executive Director
Dreamspinner Press

BA Tortuga

TWO OF A KIND

PUBLISHED BY

Published by
DREAMSPINNER PRESS

5032 Capital Circle SW, Suite 2, PMB# 279,
Tallahassee, FL 32305-7886 USA
www.dreamspinnerpress.com

This is a work of fiction. Names, characters, places, and incidents either
are the product of author imagination or are used fictitiously, and any
resemblance to actual persons, living or dead, business establishments,
events, or locales is entirely coincidental.

Two of a Kind
© 2018 BA Tortuga.

Cover Art
© 2018 Alexandria Corza.
http://www.seeingstatic.com/
Cover content is for illustrative purposes only and any person depicted
on the cover is a model.

Paperback ISBN: 978-1-64108-102-3
Digital ISBN: 978-1-64080-725-9
Library of Congress Control Number: 2018934246
Paperback published September 2018
v. 1.0

Printed in the United States of America
∞
This paper meets the requirements of
ANSI/NISO Z39.48-1992 (Permanence of Paper).

BA TORTUGA, Texan to the bone and an unrepentant Daddy's Girl, spends her days with her basset hounds, getting tattooed, texting her sisters, and eating Mexican food. When she's not doing that, she's writing. She spends her days off watching rodeo, knitting, and surfing Pinterest in the name of research. BA's personal saviors include her wife, Julia Talbot, her best friend, Sean Michael, and coffee. Lots of coffee. Really good coffee.

Having written everything from fist-fighting rednecks to hard-core cowboys to werewolves, BA does her damnedest to tell the stories of her heart, which was raised in Northeast Texas, but has heard the call of the high desert and lives in the Sandias. With books ranging from hard-hitting GLBT romance, to fiery ménages, to the most traditional of love stories, BA refuses to be pigeonholed by anyone but the voices in her head.

Website: www.batortuga.com
Blog: batortuga.blogspot.com
Facebook: www.facebook.com/batortuga
Twitter: @batortuga

By BA Tortuga

DREAMSPUN DESIRES
#6 – Trial by Fire
#30 – Two Cowboys and a Baby
#53 – Cowboy in the Crosshairs
#65 – Two of a Kind
LEANING N
#16 – Commitment Ranch
#42 – Finding Mr. Wright

Published by **DREAMSPINNER PRESS**
www.dreamspinnerpress.com

As always, to my girl. I love you. BA

Chapter One

"GOOD ride, Ap!" Dean Farber slapped Dennis "Ap" McIntosh on the back when he walked out of the arena, hat in hand from taking it off to wave to the crowd.

"Thanks, buddy. It felt good."

Waco wasn't his favorite town, but they had a fine rodeo, and an eighty-point ride on his last event of the night? Hoo-yeah.

"You gonna stick around to see the concert? It's Roger Creager and Cody Johnson."

That was damn tempting, but it was only seven thirty now, and if he hit the road, he could be at the hotel in time for his regular Saturday phone call to the kids. "Nah, I think I'll head on out. I got to ride again tomorrow."

"You sure? I got beers…."

And a pretty, pretty mouth.

He closed his eyes and prayed for strength. "The kids are expecting me to call. Maybe tomorrow after the short go? I'll feed you."

"I'm in. See you then, man." Oh, there was a promise there, a smile that went beyond buddies.

He waved, then unzipped his vest as he headed back behind the chutes. Ap wrestled out of his chaps, but he left the rest of his riding clothes on. He could just make it to the Holiday Inn Express.

Daniel's kids waited to hear from him, and Ap would be damned if he disappointed him.

He made it to his room with two minutes to spare, so he chucked his hat, vest, and boots off, laying them on top of his bag. Then he hit the head. The phone rang about the time he got zipped back up and his hands washed.

He hit the Answer button. "Hello?"

"Uncle Ap! Uncle Ap! I made a… goddamn it, Bella, back off!"

"Cole cussed! Uncle Daddy! Cole cussed!"

"Whoa, guys. I'll talk to everyone, now. Just breathe." He grabbed a Coke out of the minifridge. "Hey, y'all."

"Hey. So, I made a touchdown Friday, and Julianne is going to let me take her to the homecoming dance next weekend."

"Nice! Good job, and Julianne is the redhead, yeah?" Ap settled on the bed, wiggling his toes in his socks.

"Uh-huh. She's a cheerleader. Her momma is the choir director."

"Uh-oh. You watch your butt." Moms who were involved in school were doubly dangerous.

"Yeah, she's… she's fine. I have to get a good pair of pants and new shoes for the dance. And a haircut."

"You need me to send you some money?" Trey took care of the day-to-day stuff just fine, but he liked to send the kids money directly for special occasions. Made him a little like Santa Claus.

He heard Cole take a breath, and then someone said something and Cole sighed. "I gotta let Bella have her turn."

"Okay, kiddo." He made a mental note to add some money to Cole's PayPal debit thingee.

"I have new chickens! Uncle Daddy bought a whole farm of animals, and he says the chickens are mine!" Bella always sounded like the world was the most amazing place.

"A whole farm? Like someone else's?" He blinked. Had he and Trey talked about that?

"Uh-huh. Old Lady Marin was—"

"Bella!" Amelia sounded shocked.

"Señora Marin is real sick and needed to eat and not have to take care of everything." Her voice dropped. "God, Amelia is such a prude."

"Hey, now. She can hear you, Bella." Bella was going to be so wicked. He adored her.

"Good. Anyway, one of the chickens is sick, and she's staying in my room with me."

"Wow." Hopefully in a cage. "You take good care of her."

"I am. Don't tell Uncle Daddy. Here's Courtney."

"Bye, baby. Hey, Courtney. How's your goat?"

"She is going to have a baby goat! Cole says he's going to sell the baby for cabrito, but Uncle Daddy says we don't have to."

"You tell Cole to leave your goats alone." He knew Cole would hear him. Their oldest was being a butthead.

"I will. I am going to call the baby Patrick the Greatest Goat."

"What if she's a girl?" Amelia asked, her voice soft as clouds.

"It's not. It's a boy goat."

"Well, if it does turn out to be a girl, you can call her Patricia. Amelia, honey, how are you?"

"Okay. I miss you. Are you coming home ever?"

"I am. You know I come home for Thanksgiving and Christmas." Otherwise he was on the road. Playing the game while he still could.

"Halloween this year? Maybe?"

"Amelia, enough. Braden, do you want to talk to your Uncle Ap?" Trey's voice cut through everything like a knife.

"I'm playing my game, Uncle Ap. I'm winning. Love you! Bye!"

"Bye." Lord help him, Braden played a lot of games. "Love you."

"Okay, y'all. Tell him good night. I got to talk to him a minute."

Goodie. If Trey wanted to talk, it generally meant trouble. All the little ones—and the not particularly little ones—said good night, and then he heard Trey take the phone off speaker and head out to the rickety old sun porch that the man had claimed as his own.

"Hey, man, what's up?"

The click of a lighter sounded, then a soft sigh. "You need to come home, Ap. I need some time off. I need to drink myself stupid and get poured into bed. I need to not sleep with Courtney and Amelia on either side because their asshole older brother told them the zombies were coming."

"What?" In all the years they'd done this, Trey had never asked for help that wasn't money. Not once.

"I want you to come home. I haven't been to the bathroom where someone didn't knock for six years. I haven't slept through the night without someone needing something. I haven't gotten laid. I haven't gotten drunk. I want a motherfucking vacation. Come. Home."

Holy shit. What the hell was he gonna say to that? No? "Sure. Okay. I can skip the Stampede and stay through Thanksgiving, but I'll have to go to finals." He was number seven in the top ten.

"You always do. The kids will be excited." Trey sounded utterly exhausted.

"Not always, but one way or the other, I'll come tomorrow night. As soon as the short go is over. I'm in Waco, so it will be Monday."

"I'll be here."

"Hey, you're okay, right? You don't have cancer or something?" Ap was really starting to worry.

"I have burnout. I have been taking care of five kids for six years."

"Sure. I just wanted to make sure it wasn't like you were gonna die." He shook his head. Trey had told him back in the day that he was worthless as tits on a boar hog at taking care of kids. Why would he want Ap to do it now?

"Not that anyone's told me."

"Okay. Well, I'll ride tomorrow and come on." He mourned his rendezvous, but he would make it up to Deano later on.

"Good ride, cowboy. You know where the ranch is."

"I do. I'll be home in no time."

"Thank you. I need this." The phone went dead, the grouchy old man just a giant butthead.

He called Dean right off. "Got called home right after the round tomorrow. Rain check?"

"I could come over now."

"Oh." Huh. Well, that would be something. "I have to get up early...."

"Don't we all?"

"Well, yeah." He chuckled. Dean was a persistent one.

Ap wasn't sure if he hoped Dean would come on over or stay away.

Chapter Two

TREY headed in from feeding to start his second pot of coffee.

He put five bowls out in front of the Crock-Pot, then pulled out brown sugar, raisins, milk, and butter.

All right.

Breakfast.

Now, children.

He started down the hallway, bellowing at the top of his lungs. "Good morning to you! Good morning to you! Good morning. I love you! Good morning to you!"

He banged at every door he passed.

Kids began to appear by the time he made his way back down the hall, Bella and Amelia first, then Braden. Sleepy-eyed, hair wild, they all blinked at him.

"Good morning! Oats for breakfast. School bus is in an hour. Brush your teeth and hair and get dressed." He kissed them each, went to bang on Cole's door again and then wake his youngest, who would sleep twenty hours a day if he let her.

Cole flung the door wide. "I'm up. Oats?"

"Yep. Just for you, son. Good morning."

"Morning." Cole shook his head. "Sorry I missed feeding. I was up late working on that history project. I'll get Courtney."

"No big. I remember you telling me about it, bud." He went to gather up laundry.

He heard Courtney grumbling at Cole, but that was the last one up, so he moved back to the kitchen to start the wash.

"Uncle Daddy, my button fell off my shirt!" Bella was standing there, looking at her blouse like this was a personal affront.

"Well, either fix it or pick another shirt. You're twelve. That's old enough to mend a button." He didn't have time to baby them, not about that sort of stuff.

Her lower lip pooched out. "You never help me!"

He fixed her with a stare. "Pardon me?"

"I tried to put the button on!" She thrust the shirt at him.

"Okay, let me…. Damn, girl. The button broke!"

"I told you!"

"Go find another shirt. I'll have to take this and buy a new button."

She whirled around and stomped away, and he wanted to beat her butt, but she came out dressed a few minutes later. He let it go.

"You'll fix it, Uncle Daddy? It's my favorite."

"I'll fix it. Oats."

"Thank you." She hugged his arm before making a bowl.

"You're welcome. Orange juice or milk?"

"Why does Cole get coffee?"

"Because I got tired of fighting with him about it."

Braden came in. "You don't even like coffee," he told Bella.

"No, it's nasty."

"Well then."

She rolled her eyes, and he growled like a bear and grabbed her. "I'll roll those eyes right back at you."

She squealed happily, wriggling in his arms. "Uncle Daddy!"

God, he loved them. All of them. He hoped, somewhere, their momma was looking down on them. She would be proud.

"Not so loud, Bella! My head hurts." Courtney dragged in, her clothes all mismatched, her eyes cloudy.

"Let me feel your head, baby girl." Christ, she was burning up. "Okay, Tylenol, juice, and back to bed."

"No fair!"

"Why does she get to be sick?"

"Feel my forehead!"

"My head hurts!"

"Enough!" he barked. "Y'all eat. Now. Come on, Court. You need some medicine."

She began to cry.

The sound of a diesel truck pulling up outside made him close his eyes and pray. *God, please. Please let it be Dennis "Ap" McIntosh.*

"Who's that?"

All five kids perked up.

The back door swung open a few minutes later. "Hey, y'all. I'm home."

Four kids went running, Courtney elbowed him in the balls, and one of the bowls of oats crashed to the floor, shattering.

Yay.

"Oh, now." Ap ended up on the floor, kids piled on him.

Trey grabbed a towel and scooped up the biggest pieces of glass before he went to fetch the mop.

"Hey, Trey!" Ap was hugging kids, laughing, and Trey wanted to hit the guy with the mop handle.

"Mr. Ap. How was your drive?"

"Not too bad. Weather was good all the way up. I was in Waco," Ap told the kids. "Did you know they can't dance there?"

"Cole's going to a dance on Saturday!" Bella announced. "And Courtney's—" Courtney puked all over Ap and Amelia, who began to scream at the top of her lungs. "—sick."

"Oh God." Ap's eyes rolled, which made Trey jump over to grab up Courtney.

"You puke too and I will personally roast you in your own smoker." He held Courtney at arm's length. "Cole, deal with mopping. Braden, make more oats. Bella, clean your sister off. Amelia Danielle, if you don't shut up, I will give you a reason to scream."

Then he ran to the nearest bathroom with the puking wonder.

By the time he got back, all of the kids were eating, the puke was mopped, and Ap was wearing a clean shirt.

"Oats?" Ap asked, standing to go get him a bowl.

"No, thank you." If he tried to eat now, he might die. "Coffee?"

"Got it." Ap got him a clean cup and fixed his coffee. One cream, two sugars. It made him smile that Ap remembered.

"Thanks. Y'all hurry up now. School bus is on the way."

"Yessir." Cole scooped up dishes.

He pulled lunch boxes for Bella and Amelia out and handed Braden and Cole lunch money, slipping Cole enough for snacks after football practice.

"I'll see all y'all tonight," Ap said, taking hugs as the kids headed out the door.

Trey closed his eyes, just inhaling his coffee. *Breathe.* He could do this. He could. He'd managed to admit he needed a vacation. He'd spoken to Ap. He could do this.

Silence fell, because Courtney had dozed off where he'd put her on the couch with a cartoon.

"Tell me when I can safely talk to you," Ap murmured.

"Come to my office." He led Ap to his porch, then plopped down on his recliner.

Ap sat on one of the other big chairs, the wood slats groaning. "So, been tough, huh?"

"Yeah. I need a few days. I need a break." He needed to be a grown-up, not a parent.

"Okay, man. You should have called before now."

Sure, for his own sanity he should have. Ap was having an amazing season, though, so he knew better.

"Yeah, well." What was he supposed to say? He knew.

"Thanks, Trey. Really."

"For what?"

"For staying home with them. I got a good check if you want to take off for a few days."

Ap sent most of his money home to the ranch, keeping out just enough for travel and entry fees.

"I do. I need some sleep, a few beers." He couldn't believe it had been six years since Tammy and Daniel had died, since they'd had to take on the kids.

"Sure." Ap's bright smile told Trey the man had no idea what he was getting into.

"Good deal. I just need a few days." Maybe a week. He could take a week.

"You just set up whatever you need. The kids are old enough now that I can talk to them. That makes a difference."

"Cool. Do you need a list of all the after-school shit?"

"Please." Ap looked a little panicked for a second.

He nodded and got up so he could go grab a pad. "Cole has football every afternoon, plus his game on Friday. It's homecoming. You'll need to get him slacks and pick up his girlfriend's mum before Thursday. He has car privileges for the dance Saturday. 4-H is on Wednesday for Braden and Bella. If Courtney's not running a fever, she has dance Tuesday and Thursday afternoon. Braden and Courtney have soccer on Saturday. Bella has softball while Court's in dance. Amelia has Girl Scouts this afternoon. She'll go directly from school, and Lisa Anders will bring her home."

"Does she run a fever a lot?" Ap was watching the growing list with wide eyes.

"Nah, she's just got a bug. They've all had it already."

"Oh, okay. You'll give me all the doctors and shit." Ap grimaced. "How do I not know all this?"

"You're home for Thanksgiving and then Christmas break. They don't have activities then."

"Right. I can order pizza tonight?" That was traditional.

"You can do whatever you want, man. You're in charge." He was going to get a room at the Santa Ana. He might sleep the entire week.

"Good deal."

In a few days, he might feel bad for the guy.

"I'll have my phone, if you have questions."

"I'm sure I'll have a million." Ap laughed a bit, those bright green eyes fastened on him.

"I'm sure. You'll do fine. I just... I need this."

"Then you got it." Ap was all smiles, but worry was lurking under there.

"I ain't got cancer."

"That's what you said." Ap shrugged. "It's just not like you, Trey. You're the rock."

"Even rocks crack, man." He hadn't asked for this, any more than Ap had, but he was fucking tired of being the one holding down the fort.

Ap nodded again, almost like a bobblehead doll now. "You gonna stay tonight?"

"Yeah, I guess I should. Just to make sure Court is okay." *Dammit.*

"Hey, you can go. I just wanted to catch up." Now Ap was carefully looking away, not meeting his eyes.

"With me?" He couldn't have hidden his surprise for love or money.

"Did you really buy a whole farm?"

"I did."

"What the heck for?" Ap blinked, lips parted.

"The kids need animals for 4-H, and Betty needed money." Simple as pie.

"You got notes for me on feeding?" Ap was good with the animals, at least, and not afraid of hard work.

"Yeah. I do the morning by myself a lot, although they're supposed to take turns. They all help with the nighttime feeding."

"Sounds good." Ap sat there, back to staring at him.

"What?" Did he have puke on him?

"Huh? Nothing. Nothing. I'm hungry finally. Got over the puke." Ap stood, then stretched up tall.

Lord, Ap looked like his brother, sure as shit—lean and redheaded, a little like a fox. Him and Tammy were more broad-boned, blond. Cole and Courtney looked like his side of the family, while the middle kids were McIntoshes to the bone.

"You want something? If you can't handle oats, I can make eggs."

"I'll have oats. You won't have to do much while I'm gone. I got all my work done."

"Well, you know me. I'm a lazy bastard." There was an edge to Ap's voice that he wasn't sure he got.

"You send your money home; I know that."

"I do. I'm sorry if that's been a problem lately. Me being somewhere else."

"I'm tired. I'm damn near thirty years old, and I haven't had…. I love these kids, but…. I'd never changed a diaper when they showed up." He'd been saving for college, even. Now it was too late.

Ap stared at him for a moment. "I never—I mean, rodeoin' is all I ever wanted to do."

"And you done it. And you'll go back to it. But I need a week to pretend that… to be a grown-up."

That green stare changed, flaring with something like understanding. "Go on, man. Pack a bag and hit the road."

"I'll have my phone. I've talked to everyone, told them you were coming home. I want pictures from the dance. Remind Cole."

"I will. We'll be all right." He got a gentle smile.

"Of course you will." And if he didn't get the hell out now, he wouldn't go. "Call if you need me."

His bag was already in his truck.

"You got it." Ap lifted a hand to wave him off before going inside. Never looking back. Like this was easy. Fuck.

Well, shit. He guessed it was the Santa Ana for him, along with a nap and a couple three beers.

Chapter Three

AP thought he'd done okay.

Now, no one was home but Courtney, but he hadn't let her die of fever. A shot of whatever the hell cherry-flavored nastiness Trey had in the medicine cabinet and a little bit of ginger ale had fixed her right up, and she'd stayed on the couch all day.

The other kids should be home. Soon.

The house was clean, kept up. It was a little creepy, if he was honest. There was no way so many people lived here.

He looked for the magnet for the pizza place on the fridge. He wanted to have dinner in the bag when they went out to feed. He'd never done all this without Trey before.

"Uncle Ap, is Uncle Daddy coming home soon? I need juice."

"I can get you juice, baby girl. What do you want?"

"Apple juice?" She looked a little teary around the edges.

"Sure, kiddo." If there was no apple juice in the fridge, he knew Trey kept the shelf-stable stuff in boxes in the pantry.

He opened the pantry, stunned at the sheer amount of shit in there. Christ, was Trey a prepper?

Cans and bottles, boxes and baskets. Potatoes, onions….

Juice. With an apple on the box. Boom.

Okay. Apple juice. Bingo.

He got her set up and then went to….

"Is there a guest room in here, honey?"

"Uncle Daddy made it Cole's room. He says big boys need privacy."

"Oh." Well, shit. Where was he supposed to sleep? "Do you think I could stay in Uncle Daddy's room until he gets back?"

"Uh-huh. He's nice."

"Cool. I'll just go move my bag. Are you good with juice?"

"Yes. Are you going to spend the night for reals?"

"I totally am. We'll have a slumber party." Maybe he ought to make eggs and toast and save the pizza for when Court wasn't puking.

"Oh! Oh, can we wear jammies and watch cartoons?"

"We can!" Fucking A. Ap wanted to flex and fist-pump a little. He'd hit on a great thing for her. He was sure Cole wouldn't want to do that, but maybe a bribe….

Ap went into Trey's bedroom, eyes widening at the sight of a perfectly made-up bed, a note on the pillow. Was there a chocolate too?

He grinned. Probably not. If he remembered right, Trey didn't even like chocolate.

The note was simple: *Stay in here. Sheets are clean.*

Thank God. He dropped his bag on a chair in the corner, then indulged his nosy. He wandered around the room, marveling at how little he and Trey knew about each other.

The drawers were filled with undershirts and socks, some of which had seen better days. The closet had wrapped gifts for Christmas, starched shirts, and ironed jeans.

Two pairs of dress boots sat on the floor, along with a worn pair of hikers. A couple of silver buckles sat on the dresser, one of them a championship buckle he'd sent home three years ago. He ran his fingers over the surface, polished like it was new.

"Damn." Huh. It was almost like Trey was missing him.

He kinda liked the thought. Ap chuckled. He was an idiot.

Like they had any real history—a clumsy kiss after Daniel and Tammy's wedding, a couple of amazing nights after one of their anniversary parties. Then a couple three one-offs when they were both at the same place at the same time before a drunk driver took Daniel and Tammy and both sets of folks from them in one fell swoop. Then they were parents.

Then they'd never touched each other again.

He shook his head. Okay, he had to get his collective shits together before the kids got home. Maybe he should make a list.

A list. Right. Just listening to all the shit Trey'd rattled off was enough to make him dizzy. All he'd ever had to worry on was paying bills and getting to the next event.

"Uncle Ap? I threw up."

Lord help him. "Coming, baby girl."

Oh man. Apple juice everywhere. Did they have a steam cleaner? He mopped it up, tucked her back up on the couch, and went to look for a shampooer or a spot cleaner. The garage yielded a Bissel thingee.

Lord, Trey was stupid organized. It was unnatural.

He would try to keep everything where it was supposed to be. Trey probably really did need that vacation if he was this buttoned-up.

Shame, really. The man was a jungle gym just waiting to be climbed, even now. He worked the shampooer over the hall carpet. He should talk to Trey about wood or tile. That would clean up way easier. If he went to the Stampede and won the big purse in November, they might could do it.

Who was he kidding? He sent tons of money home; why did they still have carpet?

He was gonna have to ask, he reckoned.

He needed to make that list. Ap hit Trey's office, hunting paper and a pen.

There he found ledgers, all in Trey's perfect square handwriting, bills in trays, the desktop computer, and about a zillion printed photographs of the kids, along with everything from scribbles to detailed pictures of dragons pinned to the walls.

Damn. He felt a little overwhelmed by all the paper. Doctor bills and physicals, repairs on the tractor, tax bills. Feed store receipts by the thousands. He sifted through, frowning.

A milking stool? Seriously?

What the hell had Trey bought out from the neighbor? Last year there had been cows, horses, Sancho the donkey, and a dozen barn cats besides the dogs…. Which, where the hell were the dogs?

"Courtney?" He peeked in on her. Asleep. Huh.

Dogs. Right. There have to be dogs.

He took the dirty water cartridge out to the yard to empty, and when he stepped down off the porch, there were dogs. Five of them running at him, tails like flags.

Lord have mercy, he only recognized Miss Lucy, the pit bull, and the corgi twins, Phineas and Ferb.

"Hey, guys." He sat on the back steps while the lab mix barked at him a little. He could just make out the tag. Bilbo. Lucy remembered him too, licking him until he laughed out loud.

A little pit bull—maybe two-three months old—came up, so shy, wiggling his butt off.

"Hey, buddy, can I see your tag? SpongeBob? Seriously?" He rubbed those floppy ears, glad to see no one had cropped them. "I bet Trey calls you Bob, huh?"

He couldn't imagine the stuffed shirt calling him SpongeBob.

Cute dog, though. Phineas and Ferb pushed everyone else out of the way, both of them climbing on him. He'd known them longest. "Hey, guys. Oof."

"Uncle Daddy had to have Anna put down. We all cried. Uncle Daddy too."

"Hey, what are you doing up? You need to rest." Anna had been a damn good dog. A big herding dog, totally all fur. "I'm sorry about Anna. She was a good girl."

"She was, but she's in Heaven with Jesus and Momma and Daddy."

"She is." His eyes stung all of the sudden, and Ap blinked it away.

She came to him, hugged him hard. "It's okay. Uncle Daddy promised they are happy and watching over us all."

"Thanks, baby girl. How do you feel?" Her forehead felt way less hot, so maybe puking had been a product of the spike, and now it was going down.

"Better. I'm glad to see you. We miss you."

"I miss you guys too." He tried hard not to think about it on the road, but now his belly hurt.

"Do you want to see the 'nagerie?"

"I totally do." Time to see what he was up against.

"I need my boots. There's poop."

"Okay, hon. You grab those, and I'll get some carrots."

"They like carrots. All of them."

"Do they?" He shooed her off, grinning. "Boots."

All of them. What all was out here? He grabbed a bunch of carrots, precut he noticed, and headed to meet Court at the door again.

She led him down to the barns and the pastures beyond. "Ellie and Emma are our ostriches. They have to stay in the pasture by themselves. They hurt, 'kay?"

"So I let Cole feed them?" he teased. Ap was pleased at how easy Courtney was. He had a feeling the older kids might be more challenging.

And ostriches?

"Cole does when Uncle Daddy isn't home. They aren't tame."

"Why do we have ostriches, baby?" He took her hand when she held it up.

"'Cause the lady with them wanted a new commode put in and three new lights, but she didn't say she couldn't pay 'til after."

"Oh." Oh, man. Why was Trey doing extra work? He needed to look at the accounts.

"Yeah. Uncle Daddy cussed at her because she screwed Cole over."

Cole. Ouch. Poor kid. He was trying to get spending money and got fucked? He was gonna have to talk to this woman. "So we get stuck with the ostriches? Weird."

"Cole sells the eggs. Come meet Jennifer and Yark."

"Jennifer and Yark…." He followed Court to a small pen where a couple of very stunted, shaggy bovines stood, chewing grass. Ap blinked. "They look like tiny yaks."

"Jennifer and Yark. Yark's a boy. Jennifer's pregnant."

"They're really yaks?" He'd seen the real things. They were huge.

"Uh-huh. They're fuzzy." Courtney was so damn easy.

"And they like carrots?"

"Uh-huh. So does Sancho. He's the donkey."

"He's a good 'un." Christ.

"Uh-huh. He's going to be mine when I do 4-H."

"Nice!" He'd done 4-H with steers. "Is someone doing mini yaks?"

"Bella. It's no fair. I wanted the yaks." Court pouted for a second, then grinned. "But I can play with them and love on them. Amelia wanted a potbellied pig for the house, but Uncle Daddy said no."

"No, I bet. What about Braden?" The kids told him things on the phone, but that went so fast.

"I gave him the chickens. They were hard."

He looked out over the pasture, and the place looked like a fucking petting zoo with bulls.

Whoa.

"Are those bucking bulls, Court?"

"Uh-huh."

"When did Uncle Daddy get those?" Maybe those should be *his* 4-H project.

"He's been working with Eeny, Meeny, Miney, and Moe since I was a *baby*. They went to their first... uh... fake rodeo? A turdy?"

"Futurity."

"Right. They did that this summer."

Why didn't he know this? God knew, he and Trey weren't close, but they were partners until all the kids were grown. He resented it a little, not knowing where his money was going. How much had these bucking bulls cost? How much of his hard-earned pay was in this menagerie?

Ap shook it off for now. He'd yang at Trey about it. Right now he needed to figure out feeding schedules, when to gather eggs and... milk.

"Court, baby? Does Uncle Daddy milk?"

"Uh-huh. The nanny goats—Pip and Pop. Two times a day."

"Okay." Okay, he could do this. Cole could teach him. *God.* "And you have cows and horses, right?"

"Uh-huh. Ten horses and lotsa cows, but they're not pets."

"Right. They're work." He winked at her and got a grin. "Such a helper."

"I am. I'm going to be a cowboy like Bella."

"Are you?" Bella was twelve, and she was a cowboy already?

"Uh-huh. Or maybe a ninja. Amelia is going to be a mommy and a knitter."

"Well, good for her." He was just utterly lost.

"Braden is gonna be a teacher, and Cole's gonna play football for the Longhorns."

"How are his grades?" He fed carrots and let Court do some too.

"Uncle Daddy got him special classes after school sometimes, but I don't need them." Look at her strut.

"Well, I'll have to sit down and talk to everyone one at a time about school." By the time the horses got carrots, Courtney was drooping, so he swung her into his arms for the return trip.

"I love you." She nuzzled into his neck with a sigh. "I'm glad to see you."

"I'm glad to see you, baby girl. I miss you so much when I'm on the road."

"Do you? Me and Amelia and Uncle Daddy pray for you every night."

"Oh." That made his heart squeeze a little. "I can use all the prayers I can get."

"That's what Uncle Daddy says."

His lips twisted. "He does, does he?"

"Uh-huh. He says you got a dangerous job."

Every fucking time he started to let himself get mad at Trey, Court ruined it. Trey surprised him. Ap wasn't sure he liked it.

"I do. You ever get to see me on TV?"

"Uncle Daddy DVRs it for us."

"Yay." Yeah, he'd bet Trey screened it first too. That, he was grateful for. The kids didn't need to see him get beat around.

They headed back to the house, and the house phone started ringing as he walked up the stairs. He grabbed it and answered.

"Mr. Williamson? This is the nurse. Amelia is running a fever and needs to be picked up."

"Hey. This is Dennis McIntosh, their other uncle. I'm on the list to get her, right? Trey is out of town."

There was a moment of silence, then typing, then a sigh. "Yes, yes, you are. If you'll just bring your ID, that would be excellent."

"I can do that. Give me fifteen." He knew where all the schools were, so he just needed to get Court in the....

Shit. Did Courtney still have to be in a car seat? "Baby girl? I need you to put on slippers or shoes. Amelia is sick too."

"Okay. Poor Amelia! She hates missing school." Courtney ran to the back of the house.

Ap looked at the clock—11:00 a.m. He'd been doing this for two and a half hours. He was gonna die. He trotted out to the truck, and damn if there wasn't a booster seat buckled into the back of his king cab. Phin and Ferb barreled around the corner, begging to go with.

"Okay, okay. You can ride up front and the two sickies can be in the back."

"Oh yay! Can we get an ice cream? Or a limeade from Sonic?"

"We'll see how Amelia is feeling, but a limeade might make you both feel better." He lifted her into the truck, then helped the short-legged mutts in. Luckily, the two bigger dogs were ignoring him.

Okay. School. Right. Lord, he needed a nap. Maybe the girls would let him catch a few z's.

He'd bet they would nap if he put downers in their limeades....

Was that bad? That was probably bad. Still, a nap sounded so good. He would put them on the big couch and corral them with his legs. Boom.

They arrived at the school ten minutes later. "Okay, Phineas. Ferb. Guard."

No one would dare touch this truck with those guys watching Courtney. Not to mention that they wouldn't let Court into the front seat to turn up the radio while it was off, or to turn on the windshield wipers.

He chuckled. God knew, he'd done that enough as a kid. He'd always blamed it on Daniel, of course. Always.

His gut clenched. God, he missed his brother so much it hurt. They'd been best friends.

It didn't seem to matter how long it was, how many years it had been, he still hurt.

He hit the office and held out his arms for Amelia, who sat in a chair in a room off the office. "Not feeling good, huh, kiddo?"

"Uh-uh. I'm sorry. I didn't mean to." She was near tears already, and by the time she hurtled into his arms, she was sobbing.

"Shh. It's okay, honey. I knew with Courtney being sick, it might happen. How's your tummy?" He didn't want her to puke in the truck.

"Okay. My head hurts, though. Bad."

"Mr. McIntosh? I gave her some Tylenol to get her fever down."

"Thank you." He smiled at the... nurse? "I'll get her to the doctor tomorrow if it hasn't run its course. Do I need to sign her out?"

"Yes, please. You'll show your ID in the office there."

"Thanks." He moved back to the main office so he could show his license before taking her out to the truck.

Courtney waved at them, and Amelia waved back listlessly.

Poor baby. He lifted her into his arms, then helped get her settled in the truck. The corgis sniffed and snuffled but didn't try to get back there.

"Courtney wants a Sonic limeade. Do you want anything, Amelia?"

"I'd like a limeade, yeah. No cherry."

"Okay." He would get a couple of small limeades and some tots for him and the puppers. He rolled out, noting little things that had changed along the way. The town was growing slowly, but it was growing. There was a Michael's now, a big Albertson's. Damn.

The Sonic hadn't moved. Thank God. He got the girls limeades, then got himself onion rings and cheese sticks instead of tots. He'd split a cheese between the pups. Ferb was allergic to potatoes, and he was damn glad he remembered now. Not when the runs started.

By the time he got the girls home and settled on the sofa, he felt like he was fixin' to fall over. "You two all good?"

"Yessir. Sorry." Amelia looked miserable.

"Honey, just rest, okay. Can I lay my head back and nap?" He was sinking fast.

"Uh-huh. We can watch *Barbie*." Courtney climbed into his lap. "Hold me?"

"You bet. Amelia? You can come lean on me if you want." He wanted her to. He needed to be close to them.

Amelia cuddled into him, her poor body burning up.

He wrapped them both close before letting his eyes close. If something happened with either girl, he'd know it.

Now, he just needed a little rest.

Chapter Four

TREY hadn't made it far. Hell, he could see his ranch from his room at the Tamaya resort. Still, it felt so good to relax, to walk around naked, to have a beer at noon.

Now he just had to figure out what to do with himself.

He shook his head. Who was he kidding? Sure, he wanted the time off, but now he was missing the time with Ap. He only got a few weeks a year, as it was.

He couldn't hardly go home after throwing a hissy, though, could he?

And he didn't have a single idea how to get him a little strings-free nookie either. He'd been trying to figure out how to get some of that for six years. God, he'd loved touching that hard little muscled body.

There was something about losing your sister and getting custody of her kids, sharing it with your former fuckbuddy and brother-in-law, fighting with the law, with the schools and the banks and the kids themselves....

His whole life revolved about different things now.

Hell, his whole life was raising shit. Trey thought Ap's was not coming home.

Still, he was.... He'd been gonna have a life too, hadn't he?

Trey shook his head. No feeling sorry for himself while on vacation. He slugged another beer back and then went to take a long, hot bath.

The steam made him breathe easier, and if that made it to where he could picture Ap's naked self, well, so be it. That was between him and his prick.

He sank into the water, moaning as it immediately released some muscle tension. Oh, that was better. Way better.

Sighing, he grabbed a washcloth but then dropped it in the water. Screw it. He had unlimited hot water here, so he could wash up good after his soak.

His phone started to ring, and he flailed as he tried to reach for it on the toilet lid.

Damn near dropping it in the tub, he clicked Answer. "Hello?"

"Trey? Hey, buddy, I hate to bother you...."

Oh, for fuck's sake. "What's wrong?"

"Nothing major. Amelia has the same crud as Court. I'll take them both in tomorrow if they're not better, but I need to make sure I know where to take them. Do you have all that written down? Cole knows all the feeding and milking, right?"

"Is she puking?" *Goddamn it.* He sat up. "They go to the El Pueblo. I left their insurance cards on the desk. Do you need me to come home?"

"No. No, I just need to know what the heck to do with goat milk and why are there ostriches?"

"You chill it and drink it or put it on cereal. The ostriches were payment for some work Cole and I did." Because he'd taken them from that bitch who'd tried to shaft them.

"Okay. Amelia has a much higher temp than Courtney. Is it safe to give her more Tylenol? They gave her one at school."

"What time? You can give her a warm shower." He pushed up out of the tub. He needed to get home.

"They called at about noon. Are you okay?"

"Just trying to get out of the tub. What time is it now? Three? Three thirty? That's fine. Everyone but Cole should be home soon."

"When does Cole come?"

"Six. Football, remember? Did Amelia let Lisa know she wouldn't be at Girl Scouts?"

"Not that I know of. Who do I call?" Ap muffled the phone, and he heard voices, then Ap was back. "Sorry. I want to help, man. I just need to know where everything is written down."

"All the lists are in the office, and I texted them and emailed you. I can be there in a few...."

"No. No, I got this. I'm just not as organized as you." Ap chuckled. "I gotta go get some Tylenol for our girls."

"I.... Are you sure?" He was dripping on the mat, on the clean towels.

"I am. Really. Sorry, man." Ap hung up before he could say another word.

"Seriously?" He'd wasted his bath, his cold beer, and his hard-on.

He glanced at the bathroom, then grumbled. "Dinner. I'll order room service and have an early dinner."

Then he would head to the casino and leave his phone up here. Dammit. Ap had to sink or swim.

He called down for a burger and fries with extra green chile. And carrot cake. Hotels always had the best carrot cake. This one had caramel in it.

Trey peered at his phone, the urge to call and make sure the girls were okay huge.

Ap would call him if it was bad. The man wasn't irresponsible. He knew damn well Ap slept in the camper on his truck most of the time and ate more peanut butter sandwiches than fast-food hamburgers. The man sent every bit of money he made home.

Christ, Ap was as committed to those babies as he was.

Well, maybe mostly as much as he was.

He chuckled, pulling on a pair of soft shorts so he wouldn't shock the server when he or she came.

Supper. Then the casino. Maybe he'd get lucky.

One way or the other, he was leaving his phone up here.

Chapter Five

"COLE! I think she sprang a leak!"

Ap was trying to milk goats. Cole had walked him through it all the night before, and Ap had paid close attention. Now, though, he was utterly grateful Cole had gotten up half an hour early to walk through it all with him again. There was something wrong with this damn goat.

"Uncle Ap, you don't have to do this much in the rodeo, huh?" Cole pushed him aside with a grin and set to milking, pulling the heavy teats with ease.

"Hey! I'm not lazy." He laughed, though, because he was pretty lazy these days. He worked out about an hour and a half every day, got on practice bulls or broncs twice a week, and rode on the weekends.... Most of his energy was spent getting from place to place.

"Uh-huh." Cole winked over. "So, we're going to get my tux today? And pick up Julianne's mum?"

"Yep. Your Uncle made me a list." Thankfully, both Amelia and Courtney were way better. "So tell me about her."

"Oh, she's a cheerleader, and she's blonde, and she tastes like cherries."

He hooted. "Way to go, kiddo. And I promise not to call you kiddo in front of her."

When had he gotten a nephew old enough to kiss a girl, for God's sake?

"Thanks. Uncle Daddy calls me 'son,' so...."

"Would it be okay if I called you that? *Buddy* seems kinda informal." He clapped Cole on the back.

"Sure. Y'all are my family, all the way. I mean, I still miss them, you know? Sometimes I think I'm the only one that does."

"Hey, never think that." He squeezed that same shoulder. "I know the littles don't remember them as much, but Trey and I miss them every day. You ever want to talk about Daniel, I mean your dad, you let me know. I can tell stories."

"I'd like that. I know lots about Momma because Uncle Daddy grew up with her."

"And he's been here." He fought off the guilt. "All right, let me try the other lady here."

"Well, he's just... he just works all the time. He's not special like you, huh? I remember that about Daddy too. That he was exciting, and Momma was the one who did the boring stuff."

That was kinda like a blow to the gut. Poor Trey. If the kids thought he was dull, then he really needed this vacay.

Cole poured the milk into a container and got it into a bucket of ice. Apparently goat's milk got funky if you didn't keep it super cold. The things you learned from your sixteen-year-old nephew.

"So, is it cool if I come to the football game Friday?"

Cole looked at him. "Well, yeah. Everybody comes to every game. Uncle Daddy's coming, right? He's never missed one."

"I bet he is. He said he'd only be gone a day or two." Ap made a note to himself. *Text and ask.*

"Oh, good. He's always there. Every game, even the away ones."

"He's a good guy, huh?" And making Ap feel very... absent.

"He's a good dad. Like a really good one."

"I like how you talk about him, Cole. I really do."

Cole pinked, shrugged, but he thought the kid looked pleased.

"Okay, you need to go get ready for school, huh? I can finish up."

Cole nodded, grabbing the milk to take with him. "You want me to make oats for breakfast?"

"Could you? I swear, I'll make a bang-up Sunday breakfast."

"Sure. I know how. Peach okay?"

"It's fab. You rock." He finished up the feeding, then checked the one llama's hoof and packed it with salve. Trey'd kill him if he let that—

"Uncle Ap, watcha doin'?" Bella popped up in her little cowboy boots. "Can I help?"

"Hey. You feeling better?" He was letting her and Amelia stay home again, but he knew she was out of the woods.

"That was Courtney, Uncle Ap." She rolled her eyes at him. "I'm fine."

"Oh poop. Sorry, hon. Can you check the yaks?"

"Uh-huh. Yark! Jennifer! Come get your.... *Uncle Ap*! *Hurry*!"

He came running, because she could really shriek. "What is it?"

"It's a baby! It's bloody! Fix it!"

Oh, fuck a duck sideways. Jennifer the yak had gone ahead and had her baby. "Does Uncle Daddy have a room in the barn where he keeps meds and stuff?"

"Uh-huh." She just stared.

"Where is it, honey?"

"Huh? Oh! Here. It's locked." She climbed up a little rickety ladder and pulled out a key ring.

"Okay." He took the key. Hopefully Trey had some toweling in there.

"What do we need, Uncle? What do I do?"

"We need to wipe it down and get it warm, honey. Slow and steady so we don't scare Jennifer into defending him." He remembered this like riding a bike. Or falling off one.

"Towels. Right. Blankets? Horse blankets? It's so tiny!"

"Towels and yeah, an old blanket." He sent her off, laughing. The baby miniature yaklet was the tiniest thing he'd ever seen, and he was glad to see Mama licking the little one clean. She wasn't as strong as a full-size yak, though, so he would just see if she needed help.

Bella and all the others came rushing in with every towel from the house, plus the blankets from the sofa, two comforters, and what looked like Trey's winter coat.

"Hey, now, no couch blankets or bed stuff." He shook his head. "And no dropping them on the ground. I'll take that one, Bella."

"Oh…. Uncle, look!" Courtney's eyes were big as saucers.

"I know, right?" He grinned, because even Braden, who'd barely spoken to him, was wide-eyed and happy. "Who usually feeds these guys?"

"Bella. They're hers."

"Then, Bella, see if mama yak will let you get in there and gently rub the baby with a towel, and I mean *gently*."

"Okay." Bella's chin firmed up, and she slipped into the pen, towel in hand. "Hey, Jennifer. Hey, girl."

The mama yak put herself between Bella and her baby. Ap tensed, but Bella just stared the mama down. "Stop it. I'm here to help. I just want him to be okay. He's so pretty and fuzztastic."

He was proud of how calm she kept her voice. She moved slow and easy around to one side, and damn if the yak didn't let her in.

"Good job, Bella," Cole whispered. "That's it."

"There, see?" Bella began rubbing the calf with a piece of soft towel.

"Gentle, sweetie. Just make sure he's dry." He needed to make sure the baby got to his feet and started nursing.

"Okay." She bit her lip in concentration, talking to Jennifer all the time. As soon as she backed away, the teeny critter stood up on shaky legs, hunting its breakfast.

"All right, Bella. Guide him to the teat. Gently."

"Okay…. Little baby, come get your breakfast. How will he know how to suck?"

"They know that before they even open their eyes, baby girl."

"Really? They just know?"

All the kids were watching him, fascinated.

"Yep. That's it. Easy. Don't make his first contact with you scary."

"I promise to be nice, little one. I'm a good guy. I'm a cowgirl." God, the cuteness.

"She's gonna be, anyway," Cole murmured.

"She is." She was a natural. He was so proud. He looked around, then looked at his watch. Well, shit. "Cole, are you gonna get to school on time?"

"Yeah. Yeah, I got to go. See y'all later." Cole took off at a run.

"The rest of you guys. You want to stay home and help out or go to school?" He would call in for everyone if he had to. Cole had that football thing and couldn't miss a day the week of homecoming.

"We want to help!"

There was a burst of noise, and the little yak cowered.

"Shhh." He backed away. "Bella, get that horse blanket and set it up under their lean-to. Give them a nest. Everyone else needs to take the sheets and all back to the house. I'll call the schools. Bella, give them space, okay? No getting kicked."

That calf was eating well and was gonna be just fine.

"Yes, sir." So good. God, they were amazing, these kids.

Amelia and Courtney and Braden dragged off blankets, and he winced. He had some washing to do. He made sure Bella was in a safe place, then headed up himself. He found his phone to text Trey.

Jennifer had a calf.

Ap called the schools and explained that a stomach bug was going around. Thank God for all of Trey's notes.

"We want to go back to the barn!" Amelia and Courtney were out of their school clothes and in old T-shirts and jeans.

"Sure." He looked at Braden.

"Oats and a nap." Braden smiled. "I'm sleepy."

Ap chuckled. "I have my phone this time. No burning yourself on oats." God, he needed coffee.

"You want me to bring out a thermos of coffee?" At his surprised look, Braden shrugged. "You look like Uncle Daddy."

"Do I?" That made Ap smile. "If you don't mind, I'd appreciate it."

"Do you like Sweet'N Low?"

"Just a few splashes of milk, buddy. Thanks." He rounded up the girls to head back to the barn.

Bella was changing out dirty hay like a champ, singing Miranda Lambert at the top of her lungs. Yeah, this girl was a cowboy.

The mama yak had herded the calf back to where the blankets were wadded up, protecting him. "Slowly, ladies. One at a time."

"Is the baby a boy or a girl? Can I hold him? I want to pet him! Can we play with him?" The questions came from the little girls, hard and fast.

"Shhh." He made the universal finger-to-mouth motion. "Mama Yak has had a lot of physical stress. Like when you and Courtney were sick, Amelia. She needs to be able to rest, so we have to be quieter."

"Oh. Should we go get the eggs and let her sleep?"

Did Trey let the little girls in the henhouse? What if there were skunks and snakes?

"Uh—"

"I can check for bad things and get the rooster separated." Braden came to him, handing him coffee. "Then they can gather."

"No nap?"

"I got all day." Braden was so like Trey. So much. It made him grin. Bella, now—she was going to be his girl. Court too, he thought. Amelia was her own girl, down to the bone.

"Thanks, buddy. The help is great." He was letting them see he could use help without letting them see him sweat. He thought.

"Sure. Can we have burgers for lunch? Like real greasy cheeseburgers?"

"We totally can." If the girls were still a little off, they could have something less whoa, but he was willing to give a little.

"Cool. Come on, little girls. I'll get Evil Eddie out of the way."

"Thanks, Bubba!" All three girls tripped along behind Braden, and Ap had to shake his head. His phone chimed, and he tugged it out to look.

Hows it doing? Howre the kids? Heading home. Coffee?

You sure?

Shit, he had a feeling Trey would rip him a new one for letting the kids stay home.

Already in my truck

Coffee then. Pls

His heart kicked into a heavy, hard beat. Trey— well, it was complicated, but he wanted to see the guy.

k

Fuck. Fuck. You know what? No. No, Trey left him to deal; he was dealing. It had been three days, and no one had died. He was fine, and he wasn't gonna act like a naughty kid.

Trey could come home anytime he wanted, but he wasn't gonna scream and flail, and Ap wasn't gonna be worried.

He wasn't gonna feel like a kid getting checked up on either, dammit. This was just as much his place as Trey's. More. He paid for everything, didn't he? He was the one living on Frito pie and cheap beer.

He set his jaw and marched off to do the last of the feeding. The damn ostriches had to eat too.

Motherfucker.

Chapter Six

TREY pulled into the driveway, a caramel something or other and his mocha latte sitting beside him. He'd slept and gambled all he could, and he was ready to come home. Breathe a bit. See his babies.

He wasn't about to miss Cole's first homecoming dance playing varsity and having a girlfriend. Not a chance.

He grinned a little at the sight of Ap's truck sitting in the space by the back kitchen door. He had a deep feeling that the idea of Ap being home was going to be easier than the reality.

Still, a man could dream, couldn't he?

He headed toward the barns, frowning at the sight of the kids in the chicken coop. It was a school day.

"Uncle Daddy!" Courtney waved madly. "Braden got rid of the rooster."

"Good deal. Be careful with them eggs. Are you sick?"

"Not anymore! We're having a baby yak day! Uncle Ap says so!"

A baby yak day. Christ. Cole had better not have taken a damn yak day.

"Where is Uncle Ap?"

"Ostriches," Braden said, leaning against the fence by the chicken coop.

"You're all taking a yak day?" he asked, and Braden shook his head.

"Not Cole. He's got football and all the spirit, well, stuff."

"Uh-huh. Well, enjoy it. Tomorrow's back to normal."

"Yeah." Braden gave him a smile that was way too old for a thirteen-year-old. "Gonna nap."

Little shit.

"Sounds good."

"Uncle Ap promised burgers too."

"Spoilt brats."

Braden grinned at him, eyes twinkling in the sun. "Yessir."

He shook his head, trying not to build up a head of steam. He found Ap watching the ostriches eat, his face a study in surprised disgust.

"Coffee." He held out the caramel one. "What's wrong?"

He left off the "asshole." It seemed strong to start out with.

"These guys are just... wow." Ap smiled for him, making him blink. "Thanks. Jenny calved."

"I didn't expect that. How's it doing?" *How big is it? Is it a cow or a bull?*

"He's great. Already suckling madly. He's just tiny."

"Bella's got to be tickled shitless. I'm gonna check him out."

Damn, he was hoping for a cow. Still, healthy was better than having to take it out to the pasture and shoot it. Not to mention he might be able to sell it.

"I'll come with. Cole went to school, but I called in everyone else." Ap was looking a little… stubborn now.

"I noticed. I talked to Braden and Court. I assume Bella and Amelia are in the house?"

"Well, they were in the chicken coop." Ap started moving fast, boots kicking up dust.

Trey watched him go, chuckling softly. Oh, this was good. Really good.

Almost as good as his coffee.

Ap careened around the corner, and Trey followed, feeling like Pepe Le Pew, just wandering along, doo doo doo. The girls were with the baby yak.

Bella was holding Amelia's hand, both girls sitting in the hay a goodly way from Mama and Baby. When he walked in, Amelia burst into tears.

"Uncle Daddy! You came back!" Then she flew into his arms.

"I did! I wasn't gonna miss Cole's game, baby girl. You know that." *Silly girl.* He hugged her tight. "Like I could leave y'all for anything."

"I missed you." She snuffled and clung. When he glanced up, Bella was staring at them, nose wrinkled up.

"How's your new yak, Miss Bella?" She had nothing but disdain for her emotional little sister.

"He's so pretty, Uncle Daddy! And so strong already. I want to teach him to pull a cart!"

"I bet you can, in the spring. Did you get the wet hay out of here and in the wheelbarrow? I don't want to draw coyotes."

"Yessir. I put it with the trash you said you were going to burn, but it's still in the wheelbarrow if you want me to move it."

She was amazing.

"I got it." He walked around to look at the little calf, which was busily nursing away. "You did good, Miss Jennifer. Real good."

The mama yak looked pretty placid and a lot tired. He got it. Parenting was exhausting. Hell, the first year after Tammy and Dan died, he thought he was going to turn into a puddle of goo.

Instead, he'd gotten up every day and gone on with life.

"Why didn't someone stay with Courtney and the chickens?" Ap growled.

Amelia glared at him. "Braden did. He's old enough."

"Older than either of us, Uncle," Bella pointed out.

"Uh-huh." Ap looked relieved, didn't he? "Well, good."

"I'm going inside. I'm hungry." Amelia was pissed, hurt in the way that only a nine-year-old in a snit could be. He couldn't wait until she started having hormones.

"What's wrong with Amie?" Courtney asked. "I gotted eggs."

"Let me see." He knelt down and admired the half-dozen eggs. "Go put them in the kitchen. Good job."

"Okay. I won't run." She headed off, carefully balancing the basket.

Ap sipped the coffee Trey had handed him. "Oh, that's good. We should all go have some food."

"Y'all didn't eat? Did Cole?" God knew that kid had two workouts before he got home.

"Cole made breakfast and had some, and I made a bag lunch with an extra sandwich for him last night," Ap murmured.

"Good deal. He works his ass off, that boy."

"He does. They're good kids." Ap walked next to him, never quite looking at him.

"Yep. For the most part. Bella! Come eat!"

"But—"

"Now!"

"Yessir."

Bella streaked past them like a lightning bolt. Lord, that girl was all legs.

Ap glanced at him sideways finally. "You pissed?"

"Nope." He didn't let them argue. He didn't have the luxury of that shit.

"No, I mean at me. For letting them have a day off. We were just totally discombobulated."

He thought about it, but fuck, how many days had Cole missed until he'd got his feet under him? "I'll forgive you, man. This once."

"Thanks." Ap snorted. "I'm totally out of my league."

"No one's dead. That's a win." At least usually. He walked into the kitchen, where four of the thirteen-and-under set were making oats.

No one was dead. Still. Or burned. The eggs were where they belonged. Hallelujah.

"So what's happened since I was gone?"

"There was a baby yak. The girls had a stomach bug. Cole and I are going to get his tux and mum. Are mums still butt ugly?"

"Depends on who you ask, I guess. They're sure more expensive."

"Damn." Ap shook his head. "I guess they all need the hoopla just like we did."

"Yeah. Cole's over the moon about this little girl. It's nuts."

"Is that not like him?" Ap raised an eyebrow.

"This is the first serious one. We've had a few crushes, but this one? She met me."

"Huh. I'm supposed to meet her today for, uh, a cupcake I think. Is it true we have a cupcake food truck?"

"Yep. We're fancy now." He was going to the Range for breakfast tomorrow. By himself.

"Wow. Did Braden tell you I said burgers for lunch?"

"He did. He was excited." Skip day from school, burgers for lunch, new mini yak—the kids had to be out of their minds.

"You're coming, right? I thought we'd go to Blake's."

"Of course I'm coming. I'm not missing hooky baby yak day."

Ap peered at him, clearly wondering if he was pissed off.

Christ, was he that big of a jackass? What had the kids said about him? "I'll go grab my sh… stuff from the truck and start some laundry."

He headed outside, his head down. He needed to burn off that hay and check horses. That would require his work boots.

"You need some help?" Ap had followed him out to the porch, watching him. "Did you have breakfast?"

"I didn't, no. The buffet at the Tamaya is pricey, and I wanted to come home."

"Well, come on and eat. I can make eggs if oats are too oaty." Now Ap was smiling again. It was like a swing. Up. Down.

He didn't get it. Then again, what did he get? He wanted Ap. He wanted the little bastard to ride him like a prized pony. That had never changed.

He admired that lean, compact body as Ap moved back inside, and he followed like he'd forgotten what he'd gone out for to begin with.

What the hell was wrong with him?

He sat at the kitchen table, where Braden handed him toast and a bowl of oats. Ap moved around, scrambling eggs he'd cracked into a bowl. Somewhere, Trey had veered off to la-la land.

"Uncle Daddy, did you have fun on your vacation?" Amelia asked.

"I did, but I wanted to come home. I missed y'all."

"We missed you too! Uncle Ap doesn't know how to divide the TV time!"

"Does he not?"

"Nope. Cole tried to help, but Braden hogged." Courtney was happy to throw her brothers under the bus if it got her in good with Amelia.

Amelia nodded happily. "He was a butthead."

"I was not," Ap shot back, then laughed when Amelia squealed.

Amelia went to Ap when the man opened his arms. "Love you, Uncle."

Bella rolled her eyes. "Can I go back to the barns, Uncle Daddy? Please?"

"If you're careful. Take one of the walkies with you." They had a ton of little walkie-talkies set to the same frequency. Easier than phones.

"I will. I'll see you out there." And she was gone.

Courtney stared between the door and Amelia, over and over.

"Why don't you and Ames go watch Princess Sofia?"

"Can we watch *Moana*?" Amelia asked.

"Sure, baby. That's fine."

"Yay! Amie, come help me set up the TV!" They thundered off, giggling.

He pushed away the oats. "Smells good."

"I can make some sausage too."

"Please. I didn't even get my bag. Christ, I swear I didn't drink all that much." A few beers, not even enough to be a thing.

"Huh?" Ap's eyebrows both went up. "I don't care if you swam in a pool of beer, man. Taking time off always makes a man feel weird when he comes back."

"Yeah. I wonder if you can do that, swim in beer." It had bubbles, he guessed.

"I have no idea. They put people in giant champagne glasses in Vegas."

"Yeah? That's all cool." He stood up and headed for the truck again. He didn't need to be imagining Ap's little ass in a champagne glass.

"Uncle Daddy?" Braden followed him this time. "What can I do to help?"

He smiled at his youngest boy. "Help me unload the car? I got y'all some goodies."

He'd stopped and found the three little girls Pendleton blanket horses and Braden a new hoodie. Cole he'd found a pair of silver earrings for his girlfriend.

"Oh, thank you! You didn't go far, did you?"

"You know me, son. I need to be able to see the ranch at all times."

"I know." Braden grabbed his bag and his boots. "Uncle Ap is cooking for you."

"Is he a decent cook or should I be careful?"

"He's actually real good at breakfast. Cole was the one who wanted oats this morning." Braden pulled a face.

"I need to teach him omelets." Every kid should know one egg dish.

"Yep. He needs to branch out. Uncle Ap can make dutch babies."

"No shit?"

"Uh-huh. He says Gran used to make them when him and…. Dad? Daniel is my dad?"

"Yep. Tammy was your momma. Daniel was your dad."

"Cool. He says Dad knew how too. He said he would teach us all."

"That would be neat. You can teach it to your kids one day."

Braden groaned. "You keep saying that."

"Do I?" He opened the door and grabbed his bag. "I'm going to start laundry."

"Aren't you gonna eat?"

The smells coming from the kitchen were amazing. Sausage and eggs and toasted bread.

"You know what? I am. It smells so good." And he was starving, and all his kids but Cole were home. Hell, if he didn't know Cole wouldn't thank him for it, he'd pull his eldest out for lunch.

Maybe they could drop off a hamburger. That would make Cole both embarrassed and pleased.

He dumped the dregs of his sweet coffee in a mug and added another hot black on top. "Smells great, Ap."

"Thanks." Ap handed him a piled-high, steaming-hot plate.

"Oh damn, look at this, Braden. It's a feast!"

"Do I get—" Braden laughed when Ap handed him a plate.

"Thank you. I'll share with the girls if they come in."

"I made a big batch. Eat up." Ap leaned against the kitchen counter with a plate and a fork.

"You're allowed to sit at the table, Ap. I swear."

"Huh? Oh, sorry." Ap tugged out a chair with his foot. "I forget there's tables and chairs sometimes."

"I know, this whole house thing is strange and odd…," he teased.

"It totally is. No damage deposit…." Ap winked over.

"Oh man, is that a thing? I should charge Bella."

"It is in a lot of places cowboys frequent. I think we might be a bit careless."

"Rowdy." He knew all about trouble, or he had, once upon a time. Obviously he'd forgotten how to get into that.

"Ass—uh, jerks." Ap laughed when Braden rolled his eyes.

"Bella wants to be a cowboy when she grows up, you know." Hopefully she wouldn't ride the rodeo, although she could fly in the saddle already. She'd won a couple junior events.

"I know. I thought I might work with her a little." Ap said it casually, but there was hope in it.

"She would love that, if you have time." Part of him wanted to tell Ap not to overpromise, though. The man wasn't staying.

"Cool." Ap beamed, and he realized he wanted Ap to be careful on his own behalf too. If he got too close, he might compromise his ride.

Lord, he needed to stop thinking and eat. Men like him didn't have enough brain cells to worry on their… well, Ap was like a child-rearing partner or a silent partner or something. *See? No thinking. Eat.*

Braden was right. Ap was a pretty good breakfast short-order cook. Yum.

He ate every bite with gusto, looking up to see Ap staring at him. His cheeks heated, but he had damn near eighty pounds on the pocket cowboy. Eighty pounds and twelve inches, for chrissake. He needed his energy.

Ap didn't do more than smile, so maybe he was just being paranoid. This whole thing was weird, and it was his fault.

He should have just sucked it up, but that day had been the last straw. He hadn't even been able to shower without interruption.

The three nights at the hotel had been a balm to his soul. Trey found himself blinking at his empty plate. "I reckon I ought to get to work."

"I'm going to nap. That's okay, right?" Braden asked, and Trey nodded.

"Just this once, I guess. I'm going to be in the barns if y'all need me." He needed to look everything over.

"I guess I'll keep an eye on the girls." Ap kinda looked deflated.

"What are they going to do, Uncle? They're right here. No one wants to be stuck in the house." Braden was so sure of himself, still young enough to not worry about what everyone thought.

"True." Ap brightened. "Want some company?"

"Surely. I need to get out there before Bella decides to burn the trash."

"Well, shit. I'm coming." Ap had stuck all the dishes in the washer, so that was good.

"Yeah, she's got a fascination with that whole fire thing."

"Didn't we all at one time or another?"

"Maybe." Trey changed his boots on the porch. He had a bad scar from a bottle rocket that had damn near changed him from a rooster to a hen.

"Well, I did. So did Daniel. He was worse than me. Set the barn on fire twice."

"Oh Christ, don't tell Bella. She'll take it as a damn challenge."

"God no. I would never encourage." Ap chuckled. "Good thing I wanted to be a firefighter for a while."

"She's definitely a McIntosh, that girl. Court and the boys take after my people, and Ames...." Well, Amelia was her own person, and that was just fine.

"She's an alien." Ap laughed, stretching so long he looked like he was about to dive off the porch into a pool.

"She's our alien, though, and smart as a whip."

"She is. I like her." Ap squinted. "Is that smoke?"

"Fuck-a-doodle-doo." He took off on a run, rounded the corner of the barn to see Bella carefully forking straw into the trash barrel.

"Bella! You know you're not supposed to start a fire without me or Cole!"

"I was helping! The coyotes might get the baby!" Oh, stubborn-faced girl.

"I had to eat some breakfast. You got the straw out of the stall. That was all you had to do." He could be more stubborn. Hell, that was the one thing he had over his kids.

"Now, Trey...."

He shot Ap a look. *Don't you dare, man. Don't you cross me in front of my kids.* "No fire without me or Cole."

"Cole gets to do everything first!"

Well, duh. He's the oldest.

"I used to say that about your daddy, kiddo," Ap said. "All the time. But he was older than me."

"It's no fair. I don't get to be anything. I don't get to be the oldest. I don't get to be the baby."

"You get the baby yak to train. Just you." *Let her think on that.*

She sighed but nodded. "I was careful. I promise."

"Still, for a while longer, let me have my oldest little girl, huh?"

"Okay, Uncle Daddy." She handed him the pitchfork.

"Thank you. So, what have you decided to name him?"

"Bert."

He paused in the shoveling of hay. "Like Bert and Ernie?"

"Uh-huh. Yark and Bert and Jennifer."

Like that just made sense.

Ap sent him a look, all wide eyes and a half grin.

He shrugged to Ap. What did he know about twelve-year-old girls? Nada, despite the fact that he'd been the one with the sister.

He shoveled the rest of the straw on the fire, making sure nothing flew up and out. Bella took Ap's hand and led him back to the horse barn, chattering away about her barrel horse.

"She's so pretty. I love how deep her chest is." Listen to Ap talk about confirmation.

He had to wonder what Ap was going to do when he got tired of rodeoing. Would the man want to come here? Where else would he go?

Trey had joined his land with Tammy and Dan's, but what if Ap wanted it back?

God, his head hurt.

"Hey, you look wore. Why don't you go nap like Braden? I got this." Ap nodded toward the house.

"I think I must have slept myself stupid over the last few days."

"You still look tired." Ap said it low, glancing at Bella, who was singing to her horse.

"Do I? I didn't do anything strenuous." Hell, he'd done precious little that was fun.

"No, I just think you're worn-out. Long-term."

"Yeah, it's been a long few years." He hadn't asked for these kids. He loved them desperately, but it hadn't been easy.

"I see that." Ap snorted. "We got some shit to talk about, but not now. Go be one with the mattress."

"All right. I can do that. That hay is burning pretty easy, but it's hot deep in the barrel."

"Man, I'm not a kid. I know that fire is hot."

"Right." Christ. He headed into the house and went right for his recliner, plopped down. In two seconds, Courtney was in his arms, her thumb in her mouth.

"Shhh." He stroked her back, then eased her thumb down. They were working on that. "I got you, baby girl." He said it low, because Amelia was sound asleep.

"Love you, Uncle Daddy. Missed you so bad."

"Oh, I missed you. Shh. Let's watch our movie." He didn't even care what it was. He was home with his kids. Crazy as it made him, this was where he belonged.

Chapter Seven

AP knocked on the door to Trey's office. The kids were all gone to school, the feeding was done, and he knew Trey was in there paying bills. He'd taken the whole stack of papers from the kitchen counter and disappeared half an hour ago.

So maybe it was a good time to chat about why paying the bills was so hard.

"Come on in, man." Trey had been sleeping on the recliner for two nights, and Ap could see the tired lines written deep in Trey's tanned face. "I was just trying to get some bills paid before tonight's game. Cole's pissing himself with excitement."

"I bet he is." He sat on the edge of the weird old extra chair. Shit, he remembered this from his folks' house—the ugly orange thing looked like a monster, but it was so comfortable. "You ought to sleep in the bed with me, man. I share a bed nine nights out of ten on the road and manage not to molest anyone."

"Not anyone? That seems unfair."

"Well, if I'm gonna do that, I make plans ahead of time." He winked, pleased he and Trey were at least making an effort. It had been easy once upon a time. "Now, don't get all mad, but I got to ask. Why are you trading and working extra jobs? The money I send home ain't doing it?"

"What? That money's for the kids. I don't use it."

"The kids? So you use it to buy clothes and school supplies?" There was no way that spent all his earnings.

"College funds. Here." Trey pushed over a ledger, numbers marching along in neat little rows. Jesus. All that money was just sitting there. He could see the pattern easily. Cole's account had been filled first in a balloon sort of pattern, with smaller amounts to the younger kids. Then the deposits for Braden had risen, then Bella.

"Shit, Trey. Some of this could have gone to living expenses."

"I wanted to make sure they were taken care of."

"While you work into an early grave?"

"What?" Trey looked at him like he'd lost his mind.

"You're exhausted! Any fool can see it."

"I've been taking care of five kids for six years! It only comes in exhausted!"

"Don't you yell at me." He poked a finger at Trey. "I been living on rice and pintos and sleeping in my truck!"

"Did I ask you to? Upgrade to burgers and PBR, for fuck's sake." Trey rolled his eyes. "Haven't I been saving it? I ain't wasted a motherfucking dime in all this time."

"I never said you did." *Stubborn fucking cowboy.* "I just expected you to use some of it!" Cole was working, and Bella's boots looked like they came from the Goodwill.

"I'm saving it for college. They'll need it!"

He threw his hands in the air, which he figured he'd never done before. "Of course they will, but you can't pay bills with ostriches."

"I do a fairly good job."

"Oh, Trey, I didn't mean you don't." He leaned forward and stared into those blue eyes. "I just couldn't believe you were having to barter and shit. I can—" What? Maybe he could final this year. He could hit more circuit finals too.

"You do a lot. I just…. I knew that we had to make do. I know college is hard, and it's soon. I'm working my ass off to make sure they have the chance I didn't!"

That fell between them like a turd in a punchbowl. Plop. "Well, yeah. I mean, you weren't like me." He'd never planned anything but rodeoin'.

"No. No, I had nothing to offer but… this."

Ap frowned. "Stop that. You run this place, and you keep those kids going. I did it for three days and I couldn't see how you keep it together." Ap wasn't gonna let Trey put himself down. "I meant you were going to go to school and all. I was never anything but rodeo trash."

"You're the one that made good, and you know it."

He scoffed. "I'm getting long in the tooth. Then what am I gonna do? I mean, I'll try to hold on and get Courtney through school…."

"You know she's got eleven years, right? I mean, seriously."

"I know." He spread his hands. "What else am I gonna do?"

"I was gonna ask you that."

Oh. Well, okay. He chewed his lower lip. "I got nothing. Maybe I could—" Could what? He wasn't exactly skilled.

Trey looked at him, just still and quiet and waiting.

"I'm pretty handy with tack, I guess. I always liked to work leather."

"Are you coming back here, you think?"

"I am." That much he knew. Home was home.

Trey nodded once. What did that mean? How could there be no emotion at all?

"I mean, I could put a trailer in the back forty." Ap felt his shoulders hunch up around his ears. He had no idea what Trey wanted from him.

"Do you want your own house? I could work on that, or... I could build on here, if you want." Trey's cheeks were bright red. "I mean, I don't...."

"You'd do that for me?" Oh. He couldn't stop the grin that split his face. "I don't want to intrude. This is your place. I would love to have room, though."

"All this is half yours. I'm just... caretaking things."

Caretaking. Christ. He shook his head, his denial immediate and instinctive. "No, man, this is all you. I mean, you got a futurity bucking bull. I move back in, I'll pull my weight, but the ranch is yours."

"Have you seen him? My bull?" Trey's eyes lit up. "He's a beaut."

"I didn't look too hard. Courtney was with me, so I didn't get to check him out."

"You'll have to go see. He ranked well at the futurity. I think there's a chance this one works out."

"Have you had more than one?" How did he not know this? How did his relationship with the only family he had left get so... shallow?

"I lost a calf early on, and I had one that just didn't buck. He was a hell of a producer, though. He makes some gorgeous calves."

"Yeah? So how many bucking stock do you keep?" He knew that would include cows and all.

Trey lit up and started chattering with him, talking about the livestock, the feed costs, and land use. Some of it made his head spin, but Ap was happy to see Trey look young and engaged again. This was the young man he'd known.

Biblically.

God, he'd love to just climb into Trey's lap and rub like he was polishing silver.

He swallowed hard. This wasn't the time. Not now.

"You okay?" Trey went red and rolled his eyes. "I mean besides me going on and on. Sorry."

It was like a trapdoor falling, the animation disappearing from Trey's face.

"Hey, no worries. I like to listen." He did. He'd gotten used to it on the road.

"I get all excited is all."

Trey's phone started to ring, and he grabbed it, looking at the screen. "It's Coach Gonzales. I bet they need something for the game." He answered. "'Lo? Yessir. Sure. Gatorade and sandwiches. I'm on it. I'll have it at the stadium by five."

Ap grinned. "Parent booster, huh?"

"For every damn thing." Trey made some notes. "I swear to God, some days I feel like I got four full-time jobs."

"You want me to go get sammies and Gatorade, just point me and shoot me." They had a Subway he could call right near the high school.

"You don't mind?"

"Why would I mind? Cole's my son too, sorta. I mean...."

"He is. We've talked on it, him and me. About how I ain't trying to take away from Tammy and Dan, but he's mine and I wouldn't give for any of them."

"He said something like that. He admires the hell out of you." No way would he tell Trey that Cole thought they were both boring and Ap was exciting.

"He thinks I'm an old fuddy-duddy, but he sure counts on me being there."

"He loves you." The kids really did idolize Trey. Hell, Amelia had been terrified without him, though Ap hadn't realized it.

"He does." The surety there was something special. There was no doubt. "He loves you too; they all do. I'm just the one they expect to be home."

"I know. They were good for me. They really were."

"I wouldn't expect different. Sorry that the little ones were sick. That makes it hard."

"There was some puking, but mostly napping." Ap chuckled. "I even got to crash a few hours that first day."

"Lucky bastard. I just started being able to go to the bathroom by myself every now and again."

"No shit?" Ap clapped a hand over his mouth after he said it, because that was bad, but Trey burst out laughing, and he couldn't help but join in.

God, that was pretty, watching Trey's amusement, the way Trey's eyes sparkled with it.

He wanted. Now. Ap pulled himself together, though, and winked. "Not that I ever get to go either. Some damn fool is always talking to me."

"You're famous, Denny. It's a thing."

"Nah, cowboys are just dumbasses." And there were a lot of communal bathrooms in rodeo.

"True that." Trey sighed. "Let me pay these bills before I have to wash everyone's jerseys and two little girls' cheerleader costumes."

"Sure." He stood. "What time should I get sandwiches?"

"They need to be there by five, but I'd shoot for four thirty."

"You got it." He pressed a hand to Trey's shoulder. "Holler if you need me."

"I will. You going to meet us at the stadium or here?"

"I'll meet you at the stadium." That way he could sort of sneaky it.

"We'll all be there with our red and silver pompoms and our glittery Go Cole signs."

"Lord have mercy." He laughed but left Trey to his bills so he could go call Subway. It was gonna take some finagling to get fifty or so footlong sandwiches in about three hours. He might have to call both Subways in their area.

Go Cole signs. Christ, he hoped those kids understood how lucky they were.

He pulled out his phone on the way out to his truck to go buy Gatorade. Time to make some magic.

Chapter Eight

"**UNCLE!** Did you see what all Ap did? He brought sandwiches from Subway!"

"I did. Great game, son!"

"Thanks. Did you see me run in that score?"

"I got it on video. Your girl's waiting on you. You'd best share a sandwich with her before y'all head out."

"I will. There's spicy Italian. Is that too much for kissing?"

"If she eats it too." He handed over a mini tin of Altoids. "If y'all have sex, you use protection, son. I mean it."

Cole's cheeks went red, but he nodded firmly. "I swear. Thanks, Uncle Daddy." Cole trotted off, only to be replaced by one of the coaches.

"Hey, where did your brother go? I'd love to thank him for the sandwiches. The guys went nuts over them."

"He's over with the girls. Come on."

"Where's your youngest boy?"

"Playing pickup with the others."

"Well, I hope he's half as good as Cole." The coach's name was Mike, and he wasn't from around Bernalillo. In fact, Trey thought he was Texan, maybe.

"He's got the love for it. If I were you, I'd watch Miss Bella. She's been quarterback for her junior football league, and they've won the championship for three years." He did love his fierce, wild cowgirl.

"No kidding?" Mike followed him over to say hi to Ap.

"Not even a little."

Ray Griegos came up to him, grabbed his arm. "Hey, man. Can you come over Monday? I got some brick work that I could use a hand with."

"I'll text you tonight. I need to check my calendar, but it should be fine." He wasn't sure, but he knew he had a few days' work booked.

"Good deal. I know Juan and Hector were going to ask you for some work digging trenches. Save my day first."

"Will do."

Ap was watching him when they walked up, eyes sharp on his face.

"Hey, y'all."

A couple of players came up, clapped Ap on the back. "Great sangwiches, man!"

"Thanks. I'm glad you enjoyed them." Ap smiled, but he was still mostly watching Trey.

"Your uncle's our hero, Cole dude."

That was Ap, hero of the masses. He'd signed autographs tonight, for fuck's sake.

"Mr. Trey, can you come put a ceiling fan up in the front room? I can pay you a hundred dollars...." Miz Martinez was the head of the band boosters and one of his mentors in this raise-your-kids thing.

"You have that fan already, or you need me to run to Home Depot?" If he couldn't, Cole could.

"I got it. I just need it put up."

"Okay, I'll call you tomorrow and find a time, okay?"

"Gracias, mijo." She smiled for him, and he laughed.

Ap waited until they were mostly alone again before giving him a sideways look. "You do all the odd jobs in Bernalillo now?"

"A goodly number of them, yeah."

"Huh." Ap just stared at him a minute, then turned to nod and smile at one of the kids who came to glad-hand him.

"I'm going to go, Uncle. I'll be home by eleven, okay?"

"Good deal. You be careful. Bye, honey. You look awful pretty." He waved Cole and his girl away, his heart clenching a little. Cole was so damn close to gone.

"Thank you, Uncle Daddy!" She bounced away, hand in Cole's.

Ap snorted. "She's adorable."

"Cole's mad for her."

"I'm tickled for him." Ap visibly counted kids. "I need to go get Braden, huh?"

"Yep. Court's going to turn into a pumpkin soon." In fact he held his arms open for her. She moved into them, yawning, while Bella and Amelia chattered about the game and nibbled bits of Subway sandwiches.

"Be right back." Ap loped down the stairs, heading off to grab the younger son.

"Y'all ready for the weekend?" he asked, and Bella nodded and grinned.

"I'm going to ride with Uncle Ap."

"You sure he knows how to ride anything but broncs?" he teased.

"He has to ride around in a circle when he gets his check, Uncle Daddy."

"Uh-huh. We'll see how he does with Dandy."

"Okay."

"Daddy, I want to make pancakes tomorrow. Can we?"

"Sure, Ames. That sounds like fun."

"Cool!"

When he lifted Courtney and shifted her to one arm, Amelia took his other hand. They made their way down to meet Ap and Braden. Bella skipped alongside, singing something random.

"Hey, guys." Ap beamed at them all. "Home, huh?"

"Home!" Bella cheered. "We won the game!"

"We did. Cole rocked it." Braden fist-pumped the air.

"He did." He'd email the coach all the video he took. Everyone liked to review what had gone right as well as wrong.

"Trey! Trey, you and Cole want to come move wood for us? There's a fifty-dollar bill in it for you. A hundred if you do it tomorrow morning." Tomas Luchero was all bent and broken, the old cowboy's hand shaking on his cane.

"I can do it if Cole won't, Uncle Daddy!" Braden offered.

"Sure, Tom. What time you want us?"

"Alba will make you tortillas and beans if you come in the morning."

"We'll be there at eight." It made him happy to see Braden willing to work on a Saturday. He'd give the boy all the money—half to spend, half to save in the bank, just like Cole.

There was only three years to save for his car.

"See you then." The old guy meandered off, whistling.

They were almost to the truck when Ap turned to him. "What the hell was that?"

"What the hell was what?" Did someone do something he'd missed?

"You've booked what? Four jobs tonight? It's bad enough you're wearing yourself out and not using any of the money I send home, but you pimp out the damn kids too?" Ap was scowling hard.

Trey sucked in a deep breath, and then he carefully set Courtney down and unlocked the van. "Go get the girls in the car, son."

"Uncle—"

"Now." He didn't yell it, but he didn't have to. As soon as the kids were moving, he turned on Ap, grabbed his arm, and moved them to the other side of Ap's truck. "What the fuck did you say to me, asshole?"

"You heard me! Cole I can even see, but Braden is just a kid!"

He snatched Ap up at the collar and punched the son of a bitch right in the nose. "One, you don't question me in front of my motherfucking kids."

Then he shook Ap, good and hard. "Two, you don't ever accuse me of wrongdoing in front of my motherfucking kids."

The shove he gave Ap was harsh, sending the rodeo cowboy skittering across the asphalt. "Three, I ain't never had to pimp anyone out. My kids know how to work for what they get. You watch your filthy goddamn mouth, you fuck."

Trey kicked gravel over, staring down at Ap. "You might can take a two-thousand-pound bull, but you ain't got shit on a daddy."

It felt good to spin on his heel and get in his van, not even waiting for Ap to get up before he took off, the kids staring at him in the rearview.

"Uncle Daddy?" Braden whispered.

"Yes, son?" *Don't ask, boy. It ain't none of yours. I've heard all I need about how Ap is the hero. I'm the one that's been here for every fucking meltdown, every goddamn parent-teacher conference, every scraped knee and runny nose.*

"Your hand is all bleeding."

"Grab me a tissue from the glove box, would you?"

"Yessir." Braden handed him a couple of Kleenex, silent as a mouse.

"Thank you. Y'all want to stop over to the Sonic, have a drink before we get home? I could have a corny dog."

"Yes, please!" Bella was his bounce-back girl, her disposition never down for long.

"Can I have ice cream?" Braden asked.

"Y'all can each have one of anything you want." He'd learned early on with Cole that he had to make the qualifier; otherwise he'd be paying for the whole menu.

"Yay!" Amelia would get mozzarella sticks, Courtney would get a shake she wouldn't finish, and Miss Bella would want tater tots.

No one could say he didn't know his babies.

No one had the right to say it, especially not a rodeo cowboy who never came home.

Especially not him.

Chapter Nine

AP peered in the mirror, sighing at the big old bruise he saw there.

He'd tried to catch Trey all damn day, but he and Cole and Braden had gone to move wood or put in floors somewhere or God knew what.

The girls were busy as bees, running here and there, driving him out of his mind with questions and curiosity. He had to laugh at them, but Ap was a single-minded cowboy. He wanted to talk to Trey. He owed the guy, well, if not an apology a concession that he should never have done that in front of the kids.

He headed out to the main house, hoping to snag a girl child. "Bella? I need to ask you something."

"Yessir?" Bella had icing from one end of her to the other.

Cupcakes. Huh.

"What's Uncle Daddy's favorite dinner?"

"Like ever ever?"

Amelia looked up from where she was adding an alarming amount of sprinkles on the "decorated" cupcakes. "I know! Chicken and trees and noodles!"

Bella nodded, and Courtney's eyes lit up. "Are we going to Joe's?"

"Um." Ap hated to disappoint them, but the effort was what was gonna count here. "I was going to cook."

Bella stared at him. "You can cook that? Here?"

"I can. If you mean chicken and broccoli Alfredo." That was actually way easier than what he'd worried it would be.

"Can we help?" Amelia asked. "We made the boys cupcakes. We followed the ingredients."

"The instructions," Bella corrected.

"You can so help me. We have to go shop as soon as the cupcakes are done, though."

"Oh, I like grocery shopping. I like the fruits all stacked up." Courtney bounced and ran to hug him with sticky fingers.

"Good deal." He resisted the urge to lick her. That would be too frickin' weird. He would get a cupcake instead.

"We have to save three for the boys and Uncle Daddy, but we can have the rest." Bella stuck a spoonful of icing in her mouth.

"We'd better pace ourselves." There had to be two dozen cupcakes. That was a hell of a lot of sugar, and he was trying to make up, not get murdered.

"Are you in trouble, or are you just being nice?" God, Amelia was smart.

"I'm in trouble, but I want to be nice too." He grinned at them all. "The cupcakes look fab."

"That's important to him, huh?" Bella said. "That the being nice is bigger than the wanting to get out of trouble."

"Is it?" Who better to get Trey's feelings about good and evil from than the kids? "Well, I want to be nice. I feel like I hurt his feelings." Which had, in turn, hurt his face.

"Yeah. That's bad. But saying sorry is good, and not doing the bad thing again proves you mean it." Courtney nodded at him, so serious. "Sometimes I wish you could just say sorry."

"I know, but my momma always said that wasn't enough. You had to mean it." He started scraping icing off the counter.

"She died with my momma and Uncle Daddy's momma, right?" Bella asked.

"She did." He didn't think on it too much, to be truthful. He and Trey had lost everything in that crash. Everything but these amazing kids.

"I'm sorry. Were you a little boy or were you old like Uncle Daddy?"

"I was old, baby girl. A little older than him. Almost two whole years."

"Oh. I don't remember you, much. From before. I guess you were rodeoing then too?"

"I was. I've been on the road since I was Cole's age." He grinned, so happy to share with them finally. It felt good.

The girls were paying attention too, soaking him up.

Amelia frowned. "Cole is not old enough to go away. He has to finish high school and go to a college. It's important."

"Of course it is, honey." He wasn't gonna argue that. Trey had taught them that stuff for a reason, he reckoned, and he would present a united front. "I wasn't as smart as Cole."

"I'm going to be a cowboy like you. I told Uncle Daddy. I just want to be with the horses."

Now what did he say to Bella about that? There was nothing wrong with being a cowboy like him, right?

"I love being a cowboy, but I know a lot of guys on the circuit who went to college to study how to take care of animals before they joined the circuit." That? That was inspired.

Her little head tilted, and damn, that was her daddy shining out of her eyes. "Really?"

"Yep. My buddy Rand has a master's degree in animal husbandry. He's a stock contractor now."

Courtney stared at him in horror, then began to cry.

"What's wrong, Court?" He was baffled by her crumpled face.

"Sister can't marry a cow, Uncle Ap! She *can't*! That's not nice!"

"What?" He thought back over the last few sentences. "Oh, honey, animal husbandry is just a fancy way of saying learning how to take care of animals and find the best land and food and stuff for them. No marrying cows."

All three girls relaxed as one, and then Courtney threw herself into Bella's arms. "Oh. Oh, good. Sister. I love you."

Bella blinked hard for a second before wrapping her arms around her baby sister and hugging. "I love you, dork. Like I'd marry a cow. I'm never getting married. I'm going to be a cowboy on the range, a hero."

"I am. I want to have babies. Lots of babies." Amelia came to him, leaned in. "Love you. Let's go to the store."

"Let's put these in a thing so they stay nice." He'd seen a cake cover somewhere. It had to have come from Trey's side of the family. Ah, there. He swept all the cupcakes under the thing. "Everyone got shoes?"

"Yep! Can we get a surprise?" Court grabbed his hand.

"What kind?" He didn't lock up because Trey didn't, but it felt weird. Living on the road, you had to tie everything down.

"A... Coke?"

"Is that a surprise?" He swung her hand, and Amelia giggled behind him. Trey had taken Ap's truck to the job, so he piled the girls in the van.

"It'll be a surprise to Uncle Daddy," Bella muttered. "We don't let the baby have Coke."

"Then we'll pick something else." He shot Bella a grateful look as he buckled Court into the car.

"I'm not a baby no more. I'm a big girl! I'm a first grader!"

"The youngest is always the baby. I always was." He got them all in, then headed out to the store.

"You were? Like me?" God, he loved that, how everyone needed to be part of something.

"I was. Your daddy was the oldest. Bella is the oldest girl, and Cole is the oldest overall." He pulled out on the main road, humming along with the radio.

"What about me? I'm not anything like anybody." Poor Ames.

"Oh, honey, you're so much like your momma. She wanted to take care of everyone, and she loved so hard."

"Yeah? You promise?"

"I do." He wanted to hug her, but he was driving. "All y'all are so special. Your Uncle Trey tells me all about how amazing you are, and I've been getting to see, huh?"

"Uncle Daddy loves us even when we're not amazing, even when we make a mess," Courtney said.

"Or fail a spelling test," added Bella.

"Or lose our backpack again."

"Even when you throw up in the car?" he teased.

"Yeah, even then, but man, it makes him grumpy."

"I bet it does. I get mad when cowboys throw up in my truck too. Even if it's because they hit their head."

"Are you going to leave again soon?" Court sounded worried.

"I don't know, baby girl. I'll have to get back to work, but I'm loving being home." Hedging. He was hedging.

"You can work here. Uncle Daddy always has work to do."

"I bet he does." And that brought him back around to what he'd done wrong in the first place. He got why a man needed to work, but how could Trey grind himself to dust when he could live pretty comfortably on half of what Ap sent home?

There was so much he didn't understand about how Trey did things. There was so much about Trey he didn't get, full stop.

He took a deep breath, reminding himself of the conclusion he'd come to last night while his face was throbbing and he couldn't sleep: he needed to get to know Trey. That was his new goal.

This man was going to be his family until the end of time. Goddamn it, they had five babies to raise. They were going to figure this out.

He pulled into the lot at the Albertson's. "Okay, ladies. Y'all know where stuff is. We need to start with trees."

How happy-making was it that they knew that. That had been Daniel, asking for trees and cheese for his birthday. Their mom had laughed and laughed and made that broccoli and cheese every year.

He shook off the sadness that always came with his family, counting girls instead. Three. Go him.

Somehow he had to make sure these little ones managed to learn all about the McIntoshes. Cole remembered. These girls, though, they needed stories.

"Broccoli with cheese was your dad's favorite thing."

"More than chocolate chip cookies?" Bella sounded shocked.

"Yep. More than pie and ice cream." Daniel could go through boxes of the cheap frozen stuff after practice.

"I like Doritos a lot," Bella pointed out. "But I like pie too."

"Mmm. I love cherry pie." Maybe he would see if they had a good-looking pie at the bakery.

"Me too." Ames beamed at him.

"What pie do you like, Bella?"

Bella took the cart, and he ended up holding hands with Court and Amelia.

"Chocolate. Always. Uncle Daddy says that means I'm going to start my period soon."

Ap blinked so hard he heard his eyelids click. "Uh. Okay."

Oh man. Three of them. They were going to have to walk three girls through…. Had Trey had the wet-dream talk with the boys?

Surely he had with Cole. Braden was maybe just getting there, but surely by now. Yeah.

Damn.

Damn.

He'd always had respect for Trey, but now? Whoa. His mind was reeling.

"This way to the trees, Uncle Ap."

"Coming, girls." Time to get the stuff to make his best suck-up meal. He grinned. Trey had to be like every other man on earth, right?

His stomach would lead to his heart eventually.

"I'M going to take a shower. I got to pick my girl up at five."

"Where are y'all going for supper?" Trey washed his hands at the laundry room sink.

"Chili's."

"Cool. Thanks for all your help today."

"I like having spending money. It makes me look good." Cole winked at him before heading in to wash.

"It so does." He winked right back, knowing Cole didn't need to see him be all awww.

He pulled out fifty dollars and went to find Braden. He was fixin' to bust with pride. His youngest boy was a hard worker, just like his big brother, and it spoke well on all of them.

"We all done, Uncle Daddy?" Braden was drinking water, flushed but smiling.

"We are. Thank you for all your help, son." He handed over the cash. "You earned it."

"Thanks!" Braden beamed. "I'll put half in savings, okay?"

"You can, but you earned out a hundred, so I put fifty in."

The look on his boy's face was shocked. "I can buy that game. Oh man. Oh, this is so cool!"

"It's nice to see something for all that work, isn't it?" He clapped Braden on the back. "Cole left already. Let's head home, huh?"

"Yeah. What are we going to do for supper? I'm starving."

"I'll call and see what the girls want and pick something up. You have anything in mind?" He was pretty good at talking so that everyone was happy. They headed out to the truck and climbed in, both of them groaning a little bit.

"Mmm. Maybe we could call in to Abuelita's?"

"Sure. Let me see what everyone else wants." He hit his hands-free and waited for someone to answer the landline.

"Hello?"

"Hi, Courtney. What do you heathens want for supper?"

"Uncle Ap! Uncle Daddy wants to know about supper! What do I say?"

"Tell him I got it!" He heard Ap's voice, raised just enough to carry.

"Uncle Ap is doing supper. Come home. We made cupcakes!"

"Well, okay, then. Ask your uncle if he needs me to pick anything up."

"Do you need anything, Uncle Ap?"

"Just tell him to get his you know what home!"

"I heard him. We'll be home in a few. Cole should be pulling up any second."

"Okay, Uncle Daddy. I have to go. The white stuff is bubbling." The phone clicked off.

"They're cooking," he told Braden.

"Should I be all scared?"

"Possibly. If it's gross, I'll go get Federico's later."

"Okay. I can live with that. Do we still have granola bars in the truck?"

He nodded. "In the console thingee."

"I'm starving bueno to death."

Trey snorted at Braden. He didn't know where Cole had gotten that saying. It didn't make any sense, but they all said it like it did.

"I am." Braden inhaled the granola bar he'd found. "Do you like Uncle Ap at all?"

"What? Of course I do. We're family." He didn't even know Ap anymore, and obviously Ap didn't think he was doing a bang-up job with the money and the kids, but once upon a time he'd considered liking Denny McIntosh a lot.

"You hit him." Braden sounded young all of a sudden. Worried.

"I did." Well, shit. He ought to apologize, but he wasn't sorry. "It's not the best way to settle differences, but it's a fast way, I guess."

"It is, but it hurt your hand." Braden chuckled. "Seems not worth it."

"It probably wasn't, and I probably should have controlled my temper. I was mad." Dammit.

"Uncle Ap took his licks, so I guess he deserved it." Braden shrugged. "Oh, better. I was too hungry to wait."

"You did a great job today. Seriously. Thank you."

"Thanks for letting me come even though Cole was here." Braden gave him that shy grin he knew so well. "I can get my game!"

"You can. We'll go to Walmart tomorrow, if you want."

"Yeah? Thanks."

"No problem." He needed lightbulbs. They got home a few minutes later, and he kinda hoped the big surprise was a catered meal.

Hell, a meal was a meal. The girls loved to cook. Well, Ames loved it.

Bella was okay at it, and Courtney was... well. Wow. Seven. Seven was young. "No making faces, even if it's bad," he reminded Braden.

"I know. I promise."

They walked into a kitchen that smelled like parm and garlic and goodness.

"Oh." He breathed deep, taking in the slight funk of broccoli. "Broccoli Alfredo?"

"With chicken from the grill!" Bella looked so pleased.

"Wow! That's my favorite!"

"We know!" Court said, launching into his arms. "We told Uncle Ap!"

"Hey." Ap grinned at him from the stove. "I wanted to make it up to you, and the girls told me this was the way."

He winced at the black eye. "Well, I appreciate it. It smells great. Is Cole in the shower?"

"Yeah. Or getting smell-good on or something by now. The girls say they're hungry, but it will sit a minute if you two want to wash up."

"I think everyone will appreciate that. Braden, go get yourself clean."

"Yessir!" Braden actually hurried, and Trey couldn't blame him. His mouth was watering.

"I'll be right back." He stripped off his boots and his shirt in the laundry room. His cheeks were burning, because all the girls had been watching him, waiting to see his reaction. He wasn't used to being behind the eight ball.

Trey threw his shirt and filthy socks in the washer, before turning to head to his room. Ap stared at him, all wide-eyed and blinky. "You okay?"

"Huh?" Ap licked his lips. "Sure. I'm fine."

"Supper smells good. I'll rub a rag over me and I'll be right there."

"Okay." Ap's voice broke weirdly, but he just smiled when Trey stared. "Garlic."

"Yeah. The good stuff." He wandered down the hall and stopped to fix Cole's tie on the way. "You have her home by midnight. I'll see you at midnight thirty."

"Thanks." Cole headed out, calling, "Save me some, Uncle Ap!"

"You know it, kiddo. You have a good time and be careful."

He went to the master bedroom, grabbed some clean clothes, and headed to the bathroom to wash up. He didn't know… well, anything.

Part of him felt like he'd fallen into Bizarro World. Part of him had felt like that for six years. Ap was damn confusing, and that wasn't helping. That Alfredo smelled like heaven, though.

He needed to just eat and then find his recliner, rest his bones, and have a think.

The girls were all scrubbing counters when he came back, and Ap was pouring pasta from the pot to the strainer. "Perfect timing. Bella, I need those plates."

"On it!"

It was like having a mixture of ballet and Keystone Cops in the kitchen. Trey sat on a stool to watch, fascinated. Courtney was nowhere near fire or knives, which he appreciated. Amelia had the plastic lettuce knife, and Bella was Ap's pinch hitter. Strangely enough, it worked. Plates of pasta, salad, and garlic bread appeared, with one saved back for Cole.

"Smells yummy," Braden said, sniffing hard.

"Come eat, Uncle Daddy!" Courtney carried the bread in a basket.

"Eee-a-la! Look at all this!" He applauded, just about as tickled as a pig in shit.

"Right? Uncle Ap says he can make lasagna too!" Amelia clapped her hands before hauling salad bowls over. "Not today, but he knows how."

"He's a man of hidden talents, huh?"

"Deeply hidden," Ap murmured, pulling out his chair.

"Yeah yeah. How's the eye?"

"Sore as a boil."

"I told him to put a steak on it," Bella pointed out.

"Waste of steak," Ap shot back.

"That's all true. Use the bag of peas."

"Oh, good idea."

"It's marked for bruises, right?" Amelia handed him a bottle of ranch.

"Yes, ma'am. Uncle Ap can put it on his face."

"It feels so good," Court said. "Makes the throbbing stop. I got kicked by the llama once. Uncle Daddy let me put it on my knee. I'll get it."

Trey wasn't grinning.

He wasn't.

Honest.

Ap chuckled. "After supper. Will someone try the pasta and tell me how brilliant I am?"

Braden slurped up a noodle. "Oh. Uncle Daddy, eat."

Trey took a bite, then groaned deep in his chest. "Oh yeah."

That was good shit. Full of salty, creamy goodness, the pasta just al dente. He was impressed.

The girls cheered, and Ap relaxed, that smile widening.

He had three helpings, filling the hollow leg on both sides. "Uhn. That was fine."

Ap was grinning to beat the band. "Thanks, man."

"I'm stuffed like a tick!" Courtney patted her belly. "Ugh."

"Me too." Lord, he was going to have to take a nap before he fed critters.

"Uncle Ap barely ate." Uh-oh. Amelia was scowling. She didn't get low-carb eating at all.

"He has to stay skinny to ride roughstock, baby."

"And you don't?"

"Nope, I can be all fat."

Ap snorted. "Uncle Daddy is so not fat."

"Like Santa Claus," he teased, pooching out his belly as far as he could.

"Santa is great, but so not sexy," Bella said very seriously.

"Uncle Daddy is not sexy, Sister," Courtney intoned.

"I bet he is to someone." Ap's eyes twinkled.

"Nuh-uh. Uncle Daddy ain't never going to get married. Miss Nanette says so. He's a batch-or."

"I am a bachelor, you're right." And he was going to talk to Courtney's dance teacher about gossiping about him in front of the girls. "I'm going to do the dishes."

Ap stood. "I'll help you."

"Are you a batch-or?" Courtney asked.

"He's a cowboy. Everyone thinks they're sexy," Bella explained.

"I reckon your Miss Nanette would say I was a bachelor, Court." Ap winked at her.

"Uncle Daddy? Are cowboys sexy?"

"Yeah, Court. They are."

"Oh. Uncle Ap is kinda pretty."

"He is." Lord, this was awkward. "How about y'all go and sit with your feet up since you cooked? Braden and I will clean up."

Braden looked at him with exhausted eyes, and he knew he'd let the kid off if he didn't bitch, which he didn't.

"Go sit, kiddo," he told Braden once the girls were gone.

"There's cupcakes for later," Ap said, ruffling Braden's hair. "I got this with Uncle Daddy, okay?"

"You sure?"

"I am. Go take a nap, huh?"

"Thanks." Braden drooped with relief, trudging off like a man pardoned from a hanging.

He waited for Ap to start in about how he was abusing Braden, working the kid too hard.

"Worked hard, huh? He looked pretty happy when you got home."

That wasn't too bad, maybe.

"He did a good job. He earned his money. I promised to take him to the Walmart tomorrow."

"Yeah, he wants that new Assassins game." Ap started rinsing plates. "Look, I was an asshole, okay? I'm not here like you are. You know how to divvy up the money."

"I'm not abusing the kids. I'm not making them suffer. I'm teaching them to work hard and earn their own money."

"I get that." Ap shrugged. "I just had this image in my head, you know. That my money was maybe getting them school clothes and movies and stuff too."

He didn't know what to say. "I didn't want you to think I misused it. I've always been careful."

"I know." Ap just scrubbed, but he was smiling. "It's just gonna take some getting used to. Putting reality in place of the fantasy, if that makes sense."

"Yeah, there's no fantasy here." No, just hard work, running kids back and forth, and long nights.

"There is, though." Ap hunched his shoulder a little. "Having a place, having a routine. I reckon it sounds nuts, but it sounds really nice."

"You have a place here." He was tired of this. Ap had a place with them.

"I know." Ap shook his head, blowing out a breath. "I suck at this talking shit. What I mean is, when you're on the road, you have all these white-picket-fence thoughts. It's all idealized."

"Sure. I bet. I wish I wasn't spending every night alone here."

"What, you didn't get any on your little vacation?"

He thought, just maybe, Ap was joking with him like he would with a buddy on the road. There was an edge to it, though.

"Shit, I don't even know how to pick someone up anymore." And that was the God's honest truth.

"I don't either." When he raised an eyebrow, Ap just laughed. "There have been some friends with benefits over the years."

"You're sexier than me, remember? You're a cowboy."

"So are you, Trey. The hardest working one I know." Ap rinsed the big skillet.

"Thank you." That meant a lot. Like all the lots.

"It's true. Even if you have an ostrich." Ap flipped a towel at him.

"And three miniature yaks." He waggled his eyebrows at Ap.

"A baby one, even. Who ate well this morning, by the way. Bella's getting good with him too."

"She's something else. She's a rancher, all the way." She was a cowgirl.

"I adore them all, but she's freaking amazing." Ap leaned back against the counter once the dishes were done. "So now that I've apologized, I been meaning to ask."

"Yeah?" He waited, forcing himself to not get all tense.

"Well, I don't want to sound skeezy, but I meant it when I said we could share the bed. It's silly for you to sleep in the recliner. I share a bed, platonically, on the road all the time."

"Fair enough. You going to be able to stay for a while?"

"I'm gonna stay through Thanksgiving, then go to finals. I'll come back for Christmas, though, and stay through to—well, I can't make any promises, but I'm thinking on skipping Denver and Fort Worth and not heading out until March." Ap looked so hopeful.

"We'll be right here. You are always welcome."

"Thanks." Those shoulders had come all the way down, relaxed.

"Thanks for supper. It was good."

"I like Alfredo. It's pretty easy, even if there are lots of parts." Ap perked right up, looking so pleased.

"I like it too. A lot. You want to come watch a show before we go feed?"

"I do." Ap came and put a hand on his arm. "Maybe close your eyes for a minute too."

"Maybe, yeah." Oh, that touch made his heart hiccup. His skin was all tingling.

"Come on. We'll watch… *Homicide Hunter*?"

"Oh, I like that." *I like you, Ap.*

"Yay!" Ap kept hold of him, sliding that hand down to his wrist. How was he ever going to sleep in the same bed as this guy?

He was going to be sporting permanent wood.

They settled, him in his recliner, Ap close to him on the couch. The girls were all asleep, their busy day catching up with them.

He relaxed, letting himself breathe, melt into the chair.

Ap turned the TV to *Homicide Hunter* after turning down the volume, then put his feet up and leaned back.

He didn't even make it to Joe Kenda's first smartassed comment before he was asleep.

Chapter Ten

AP stepped out of the bathroom, a billowing cloud of steam following him like ghosts. God, he'd needed that. Really, really.

He'd put hand to cock, and he was feeling loose-limbed and easy in his skin. Damn, that felt good, and remembering how pleased Trey was with supper made him feel ten feet tall.

Trey was in a pair of shorts and nothing else, sitting on the edge of the bed, playing with his phone.

Good thing he'd worn a towel. He smiled, glad Trey was ready to come back to his own room. "Hey. Did I hog the bathroom?" Trey had showered after feeding, saying the washcloth hadn't done it.

"Nah, I was just wanting to sit."

"Oh, cool. You don't get to a lot." He admired the breadth of Trey's shoulders, the muscles that bunched and moved. Christ. There was nothing as hot as a big old boy. Like a mountain ready to be scaled.

He tightened the towel, making sure the hard-on that was threatening stayed hidden.

"You used my soap. It smells good on you."

"Thanks. I should have got some at the store, I guess, but I've always liked that smell."

"I like it. It suits you to the bone." Oh, that was the hottest thing anyone had ever said.

"Good deal." He didn't know what else to say, so he sat on the other side of the bed.

Trey stood up, swaying a little. "Someone had the dogs in the house."

"Huh."

Trey bent over, showing off that fine, fine ass, before coming up with a beat-up tennis ball. "Dogs."

"Is that bad? I thought Phineas and Ferb were allowed, at least."

"Only when I step on toys. They're all house trained."

"Okay." That way he didn't have to apologize for playing ball with the corgis.

"It was you, huh? Trying to bring me down?" Trey grinned at him, eyes warm, twinkling.

"That's got to be it. Trying to get you all hobbled."

"Lord, it was bad enough that time when Hobbes kicked me and busted a bone in my back. Cole was thirteen, and I thought he'd never get me to the truck to drive myself in to the doc's."

"Oh, holy shit. What the hell did you do?"

"Wore the back brace." Trey chuckled. "Wanna see? I have a hoof-shaped thing."

"Uh-huh." How had he not known about this?

Trey eased down the shorts, the U-shaped scar clear as a bell.

He touched it without even stopping to think. Ap traced the scar, thinking how lucky Trey had been that it wasn't right on the spinal column.

The soft moan surprised the hell out of him, Trey shivering.

Ap froze, hand against Trey's skin. "You, uh, you okay?"

"Uh-huh. Sorry. I—sorry." Trey moved away and headed for the bathroom, sporting a heavy, fine erection.

"Hey." He lunged, grabbing Trey's arm, all good sense going out the window. "Why are you sorry?"

"Because... fuck, I don't know. I don't want you to think I'm... but I do." Trey turned to face him, that confusion clear.

Ap nodded. "I do too."

Then he took the bull by the horns, so to speak, and cupped Trey's cock.

Trey's eyes went wide, his mouth falling open. "Oh, holy Jesus."

"Yeah." Oh, feel that.... He pressed and squeezed gently, utterly fascinated.

One huge hand landed on his shoulder, hot and solid. "Ap."

"Uh-huh. I dream about you, Trey. I have for years."

Trey's eyelids went heavy, the look pure lust. They swayed toward each other, and Ap had to take a kiss. A hard one to make up for lost time.

Had Trey always tasted this good? Had he always been so hard and hot where they rocked together? He could barely remember, so he needed to do this now to remind himself.

Trey grabbed him, hands huge on his ass. Damn. He locked his arms around Trey's neck, loving how strong this man was. Trey held him like a boss, like he weighed nothing at all.

They started moving together, rocking and rubbing, their skin hot as fire.

"I want…." Trey groaned and bit his bottom lip, making it sting.

Ap pushed Trey's shorts down and brought their cocks together, stroking as hard and fast as he could.

"Jesus. Jesus, please." Trey bucked under him, the best ride he'd had in eons.

"Uncle Daddy! Uncle Daddy! There's a spider!" Amelia's scream was pure terror.

Trey damn near killed them both springing away to yank up his shorts. "I'm coming, baby!"

Courtney started to cry, harsh sobs. "It's coming! Uncle Daddy! Save me!"

Slamming out of the room, Trey grabbed a boot. Ap yanked on his pajama pants before following, getting there just in time to see the demise of an enormous wolf spider.

"Fuck, look at that!"

"Throw it away!" Amelia was rocking, poor baby obviously scared out of her mind. "Make it go away!"

"Ames! You're scaring your sister."

"She's going to end up in the looney bin one day." Bella had that disdain that only a big sister not scared of spiders could have.

"I'm not crazy!" Amelia screamed, which just made Court cry harder.

"Here." Ap ran to the bathroom and returned after he'd grabbed a big handful of toilet paper. "Let's get it out of here."

"You get Court; I'll take Ames?"

"Yep." He took the spider carcass, which even he didn't want to touch, away. When he came back, Courtney leaped at him, wrapping her little arms around his neck. "It ran at us."

"Oh, you were so brave, then, baby girl."

"Uh-huh. I cried, but it was so big!"

He could hear Amelia sobbing, hear Trey murmuring to her.

"It was. Good thing Uncle Daddy has big boots."

"Uh-huh. You picked it up. Is that the only one?"

"It is. They don't share space." And that one hadn't had babies on it....

"You promise?"

"Want me to look?" He was never going to promise no spiders. This was the desert.

"In my bed and in Ames's bed?"

"Yep. Under too." He put her down next to Trey. "Just a minute."

Trey drew her in, and she wrapped around Amelia. "Uncle Daddy and Ap fixed it, Ames."

Amelia hiccupped. "I hate spiders."

Ap got the flashlight they kept by the door in the kids' rooms, then knelt on the floor, peering under each bed in turn. "All clear."

"Stay with me?" Court said. "Sleep with me, Uncle?"

"I'll keep watch until you go to sleep, huh?" He winked at Trey, who had to be worn to the bone. "Go on, Uncle Daddy."

"In a minute." Trey's arms were full of sniffling nine-year-old.

"Come on, honey. Back to bed." He sat with Court, humming "Strawberry Roan" because he didn't know any lullabies.

She curled up with him, this sweet little thing. "Do you remember when I was a baby? Were you here?"

"I was. I thought you were so pretty, but I was afraid I would break you if I held you too hard."

"Uncle Daddy helped me be a baby, you know? 'Cause my momma and daddy and grannies and pappies all died in a van. Uncle Daddy and you?"

"I was with you then, yeah." He hadn't been around much, because money had been so damn tight and he'd just been starting out rodeoing. God, he'd scrimped and saved back then, his chaps secondhand, borrowing other guys' rigging. "You were so tiny, and you slept on Uncle Daddy's chest for so long."

Trey had been a baby himself, and Lord, he had to have been terrified, but he'd manned up. No matter what he thought of some of Trey's methods, he had to love the guy for holding the whole family together.

Hell, Trey had become dad and mom and rancher all in the same breath. Had Trey even known how to cook? How to change a diaper?

He'd been so busy trying to make money and mourn the loss of his people that he'd let Trey swing a little, but inheriting five kids from ten years to six months old? Damn.

They'd both made mistakes.

He didn't even realize Courtney had fallen asleep until Trey eased up off Amelia's bed and motioned for him to come on too.

He stood up and headed out, then closed the door behind them.

"That was an emergency." He grinned at Trey. "We did good."

"Lord. I don't understand her panic about the spiders, I swear to God."

"Amelia? Sometimes fear is just irrational. Her gran was terrified of them."

"Yeah? You... you want a beer?"

"I do." The adrenaline might take a while to shut off.

"Me too. Come on." Trey led him to the kitchen and found them both a Dos Equis.

"Yum." He did love a fancy-assed beer. On the road, mostly he let the other guys buy, and they did a lot of Michelob Ultra because it was low cal and carb.

"Yeah. I have a six-pack a month. I'm not drinking horse piss."

"I get it." He did, but he'd also learned not to turn down a fan who wanted to buy you a meal or a beer.

They sat at the table, drinking and looking at each other.

He wasn't sure what to say. Ap wasn't about to apologize for their clench. In fact, he wanted to do it again.

"I ain't all sorry, Ap."

"No? Good." He grinned. Wide. "Me either."

"Good." Trey blushed, but there was this little smug smile.

He laughed right out loud. "We can try it again, whenever you want."

"We'll probably have to; otherwise I'm going to die of blue balls."

His cheeks heated until they felt fiery, but Ap wasn't a virgin. He just hummed happily. "Maybe not until we know they're gonna sleep."

"Yeah. And Cole comes home. I hope he's having a good time."

"Me too." Ap looked at the clock on the microwave. Cole wasn't late. It just seemed like it should be after midnight.

It wasn't. It was ten thirty. He had a couple of hours to imagine touching Trey, loving on the man for the first time in years.

He took a deep breath. *Calm down, fool. Soon.*

"Did you mean it?"

"What? That I want to have you? Yeah." He wasn't sure what else Trey might be talking about.

"That you thought about it, before."

"Oh, Trey." He got up and moved to stand in front of Trey. "I wake up sweating and shaking because of you."

Trey hummed softly and leaned forward, one hand on his hip. "You're so fine."

"Yeah? Not too skinny?" He heard that sometimes from a few buddies.

"You hear the kids. You're the pretty one. I'm a big old boy."

"You're like a mountain. A feast." Ap reached out to touch Trey's chest. "You held me like I weighed nothing. You know how hot that is?"

Trey ducked his head, cheeks pink, but that smile was something else. Like dawn breaking.

He didn't get how Trey didn't know how fucking hot he was. Ap thought he was beautiful. So damn perfect.

Lord, listen to him. One kiss in six years and he was smitten again.

He'd never really given up, he reckoned. Just pushed it all aside.

Just told himself it was all about work and money and the kids and not Trey.

He stroked Trey's shoulder, then upper arm. All that skin. "Were you all muscled like this when we were together?"

Trey shook his head. "Nah. I was a skinny kid."

"Yeah, not anymore."

"No. Not anymore. I grew into my shoulders."

"You so did." Feeling daring as hell, Ap slipped down to straddle Trey's lap.

"Oh, you…. You feel good to me."

"Mmm. Hot as fire." He kissed that mouth, knowing he was tempting fate, but Ap just couldn't care.

He felt that heavy cock filling, making promises that he needed Trey to keep. Ap wasn't sure he could take another interruption. He pushed into Trey's shorts, grabbing hold. "Jesus, man. You are a handful and a half."

"I'm big all over?" Trey laughed, the sound so young and free.

"You are. Big and strong and right here." Ap bent to nibble just below Trey's ear. He remembered that Trey was sensitive there.

"Uhn." Trey rocked them in the chair, panting.

So, right there, just like he remembered. God, it had been so long, but it seemed like yesterday, shining in his memory.

He bit a little, letting it sting enough that Trey flailed and grabbed for him.

"I got you, honey," he murmured. "You're just fine."

"That burned so good."

"Did it? Can try it again." He grinned, slow and easy, just ready to try all the things.

"Please." Trey lifted his chin.

So Ap bit down, worrying that spot with his teeth. He never spent time playing, experimenting. Marking. This was a damn fun way to spend an evening.

He dragged his fingers over Trey's fuzzy chest, tugging a little.

"Mmm." Trey leaned closer, willing and able to take anything he had to give. Damn, all this need just waiting for him.

Ap kissed Trey on the mouth again, his hand still moving between them.

"We need to… I want to be naked with you, Ap."

"Then we need to go close that bedroom door." That way no one would interrupt, like Cole coming home.

"Yes. Is now okay with you?"

"We've waited for six years, Trey."

"Is that a yes?" Trey looked uncertain, so Ap jumped up, then yanked Trey to his feet.

Trey chuckled and let him muscle him into the bedroom, where he markedly locked the door behind them.

"They can knock," Trey said when he raised his eyebrows.

"They can." He looked at Trey. "Get naked."

Trey shucked his shorts in one movement. "Ta-da."

"Jesus, I will ride you like a prized pony." He stripped out of the pajama pants before moving toward Trey, stalking him.

"I want you, huh? Bad." That was obvious from the fat cock curving over Trey's belly.

"I love that." He meant the wanting and the hard dick. He reached out to touch, feeling the head with his fingers. Trey moaned for him, and that sound was enough to blister him, to make him whimper in response.

He slid his hand down the shaft, then tugged. "Bed."

"Uh-huh." Trey stepped forward, bringing them together.

They turned as one man, sort of stumbling to the bed so they could stretch out and face each other.

"This is real," Trey whispered.

"Real as anything ever has been, honey." He leaned close for a kiss. Trey wrapped one arm around him and drew him in, cradling him against that sweet, fine body.

God, all that muscle was inspiring, and Ap wanted to touch more of it.

He felt surrounded, like Trey was everywhere, anywhere he touched. The sheets smelled like him, but Ap was happy to let their scents mingle, to mix that up and sleep on it.

"What do you want, Ap? My mouth, my hand?" The words were breathed against his lips.

"Oh God. I—" He wanted everything. For now, he wanted to see Trey's face when they came, to prove this was no fantasy. He dragged Trey's hand down to join his.

"Mmm...." Trey grabbed their cocks together, jacking them with hard, firm strokes.

His eyes rolled right back in his head, so Ap had to work to see like he'd wanted to. He just needed this so much, loved how heated Trey was, how easy in his skin.

He dove into the kisses, feeding Trey little cries every time that huge hand caught a nerve on his shaft. Trey was right there with him, hard as a rock and twice as hot.

Ap grunted as Trey squeezed, his ass going tight at the touch. He arched, pushing into Trey's fingers, letting that stroke and pull drive him to new heights. He started muttering, rough, low, filthy words that made Trey growl.

"Please. Come on, Trey. My balls hurt. Make us come. Now."

"Uh-huh." Trey rolled his palm over the tips of their cocks, the buzz and burn of nerves just right.

"There!" He almost sent them rolling off the bed when he lunged, unable to keep his balance.

Trey did it again, then again, then once more.

Ap groaned, his whole body convulsing when he shot. His balls pulled up so tight he had to grit his teeth, and he cried Trey's name. Trey kissed him, thrusting restlessly against him, over and over.

He got his fingers working, got to stroking Trey, who fucked his hand.

"Yes. Yes. Please."

So damn pretty.

"I'm watching you, Trey. I see you." He squeezed down hard.

Wet heat coated his fingers, Trey's cry trapped against his skin. He'd never seen anything as amazing as Trey's face when he came, and he'd been afraid he'd never see it again.

Ap rubbed the come into their skin, so damn happy he could bust.

"Damn," Trey whispered. "Really."

"Uh-huh."

The knock at the door made them both groan softly, but Braden called out, "Are you okay? I heard noises."

"Just fine, bud. We were changing the sheets."

"Oh, okay. Can I get a small ice cream cone?"

"Sure. No problem." Trey looked at him, and he had to fight his laughter.

Changing the sheets? Seriously? All that grunting and sweating....

"Thank you!" They heard Braden thunder off down the hall.

"Changing the...."

"It requires pulling and stuff, right?"

"Uh-huh. How long will he believe that?" Ap asked.

"Until he tells Cole tomorrow. Cole will tell him it was bullshit." Trey gave him a wry smile.

"Damn." He grinned over. He wasn't ashamed. They were family, right? "They know, right? That you're gay?" That would be a rotten thing to hide from the kids.

"Cole knows, so I can assume Braden and Bella know. I don't know about the babies."

"Cool." He thought so, at least. He wasn't going to hide how much Trey made him feel.

"Cole knew about us. Not that we had a thing, but that we were gay, before Tammy and Dan died."

"Then it won't be a big deal." He didn't want to cause drama or trauma.

"No. They're good kids. They want people to be happy."

"Good deal." He took one more kiss. "You want to watch TV for a bit? Just hang?" That sounded so good.

"Yes. I want. We'll have to put shorts on. Cole will want to talk."

"You got it." He rolled free before rising to get a warm, wet washcloth and two pairs of shorts in turn.

They got cleaned up, and Trey went to unlock the door before handing him the remote and settling beside him. He put an arm around Trey because he could. It made him feel good deep in his bones.

Trey grinned over at him, the look almost shy. Yeah. Years could do that. They had to start all over.

Good thing he had a little time to stick around right now and get a little bit of a push in.

After all, he wasn't going to disappear off the face of the earth, was he?

Chapter Eleven

"**UNCLE** Daddy, I can't find my shoes!"

"Uncle Daddy, Amelia pushed me."

"Uncle Daddy, is there more bacon?"

Trey tried not to growl, but he felt like the kids were out to get him today. Like they knew he'd had a short sleep last night, thanks to Ap.

Whoa, because of Ap.

He still couldn't believe it.

"Uncle Daddy, can I go out and see the horses?"

"Uncle Daddy, I spilled my orange juice."

"Uncle Daddy, Cole's still in bed!"

He closed his eyes and counted to twenty.

"Hey, what's going on with you guys? It's Sunday! Aren't you supposed to want to sleep in?" Ap poured him another cup of coffee.

"Sleeping is silly!" Court announced. "We want to do fun things!"

"Sleeping is fun," he muttered. "Thanks."

"Why don't we go out, then, and Uncle Daddy can have a sit?"

"Okay! Uncle Daddy! We're going out with Uncle Ap!"

He stared at Court for a second, then began to chuckle. *Silly girl.*

"Where are you going?"

"Um." She looked at Ap.

"Jemez?" Ap looked so pleased.

"Oh, are we going to the dam? Get your swimming suit!" Bella ran for her room.

"Uh, Ap? It's October. They'll freeze."

Ap frowned. "We can go to the hot springs, then, right?"

"You can. Can I come too?" He wanted to soak.

"Hell yes." Ap beamed. "I'll even buy you lunch."

"I'll see if Cole is coming or staying home." He took his coffee down the hall. "Son? We're going to Jemez. You want to come?"

"No. I got homework." The door opened, Cole grinning at him. "Nothing serious, but...."

"But someone's going to call and you might want to go see her, huh?"

"Yeah. Maybe." Cole waggled his eyebrows. "Can you believe I'm skipping Jemez for a girl?"

"Eeeee." He winked. "Of course I can. I'll leave you a twenty for Abuelita's, since you didn't get to go the other day."

"Oh wow. For that I'll dig out that trench you need."

"You're a good kid, no matter what they say about you down to the jail."

Cole snorted. "I'm a fool in love, Uncle."

"You are." He winked, then made his way to his room to get ready for the hot springs. "Don't forget to have everyone get a towel! They don't hand them out anymore!" he called.

"I gotted my Moana towel!" Courtney ran right into him. "Hi, Uncle Daddy!"

"Hi, Courtney!" She was so excited that he felt a little guilty. How long had it been since they'd just taken a Sunday to go?

"We're going to the springs! And you're coming too!"

"I am." He hugged her with one arm. "Go get your shoes."

"Oh, right!" She ran off.

"Is this okay, Uncle Daddy?" Amelia asked, modeling the past summer's bathing suit.

"We'll have to get you a new one, but it's fine, kiddo."

"Make sure to bring regular clothes too and put panties in your bag."

"Okay!" She ran back off too. Braden and Bella were already sitting in the kitchen again when he got back, bags packed. Ap was there too, sipping his coffee.

"The little girls are getting ready. Cole's staying home."

"Yeah? Is he okay?"

Ap's question might as well be "Is he hungover?"

"The girlfriend is going to call."

Braden rolled his eyes. "Gag."

Bella giggled. "I think it's kinda neat."

"Are you going to start dating Billy Garces?" Braden teased.

"Shut up!"

"Hey!" He snapped it out, making them both jump. "We're all going to go have fun today." Ap was staring at him, but he had no idea how mean Braden could get.

"Yes, sir." They spoke together, but he could see revenge in Bella's eyes.

He would have to make sure she didn't cut Braden off at the knees and drown him.

"Is that everyone?" Ap asked when the little girls came out. "Does everyone have shoes? Underwear?"

Oh, good man.

"Towels," he added.

"Right. When did they stop doing towels?" Ap asked.

"Few years ago. They decided laundry used too much of the water co-op."

"Huh. Good to know. You looking forward to it?"

"God yeah." It would be nice, both of them able to watch. He might actually get a soak.

"Cool. I was just reaching for ideas, but it sounded so good."

"It's a great way to spend a Sunday. Seriously."

"Thanks." Ap touched the back of his hand, just a tiny contact that sent a thrill up his arm.

He felt a little like he was on alert, like his body was permanently buzzed. His cheeks heated, and when Braden stared at him, Trey just smiled.

"Okay, guys, let's hit it." Ap got everyone up and moving.

They settled in the van, Trey pushing in the driver's seat. "Whose turn is it to pick the music?"

"Mine!" Bella shouted, and since no one argued, it must have been hers for sure.

"What do you want?"

"'El Rey'!" Bella had developed a huge crush on George Strait after some YouTube video she'd watched. Then she'd found out he'd covered her favorite mariachi song. Lord help them.

"Ap, can you make it happen?" He handed over his phone.

"I can." Ap hooked his phone up to the little cable in the console so it would play on the car sound system. Then he found "El Rey," and they all started singing about with money or without money....

Ap watched for a second, and then he started laughing, big, happy guffaws that rang out. By the last chorus, Ap was singing with them, his Spanish surprisingly good.

From there they moved to "Adalida," to "Hot Grease" and "Zydeco," and they were all laughing and singing and... God, this was good.

He'd been ready to kick Ap for suggesting the kids go out somewhere, but those smiles.... They all deserved a day.

Ap reached across, touched his leg, then grinned.

He nodded, turning off the road that led up to the town of Jemez Springs and the springs itself. Maybe after, they could go to Dave's Burgers and chow down. If everyone was good....

After all, Ap had promised to buy.

He grinned. Oh yeah. Maybe breakfast all day. He did love an omelet smothered in green chile.

The turnoff to the springs damn near snuck up on him, and the girls squeaked when he spun into the road.

Bella applauded. "Go, Uncle Daddy!"

"Like a boss!" Braden said.

Ap hooted again. "You've got it, honey."

"Yeah, yeah, yeah." His cheeks burned, though, he was so pleased.

They wended their way up to the springs, the little buildings cheerful in the fall sun. "Okay. No running, no fighting, and no doing anything awful. Got it?"

"Got it."

"Bella, I'm looking at you."

She rolled her eyes dramatically. "I'm an angel."

"Uh-huh. If you kill your siblings, I'm going to know."

She batted her eyelashes. "I'll wait until we get home and put yak poop in his bed."

Ap stared over at him. "Is she serious?"

"Hey, she's yours too."

"Are you serious?" Ap turned to Bella.

"Yep." She said it super cheerfully before climbing out of the van.

"I'll go pay. You are in charge of the heathens and Ames."

"Okay." Ap rounded up all the kids, and they headed inside. They were really on pretty good behavior, probably for Uncle Ap.

Buttheads, all of them. He grinned and went to pay his dimes so he could go soak his bones.

The springs was always so pretty, but today it was surprisingly uncrowded. He would bet a lot of folks thought it was too cold, but in the pools themselves it would be amazing. He'd sat in hot springs with snow falling on his head. It was a thing.

The kids played and laughed, showing off for Ap, and he just watched with heavy lids. He was warm and sleepy and happy enough that he had a permanent goofy grin on his face.

Ap waved at him, that compact body bare to the waist and so damn beautiful it took Trey's breath. He nodded, sinking down deeper. Compared to Ap, he was... rough.

Of course, Ap didn't seem to mind a bit.

He grinned wider. No, sir, Ap seemed to find him inspiring. Super-duper so.

"What are you grinning about, Trey?" Ap looked like maybe he suspected.

"Huh? Just having a good day." He was allowed.

"Glad to hear it."

"Yeah." He saw Bella floating on her back, her hair all spread around her.

"Uncle Daddy, can I sit in your lap?" Courtney floated over. "I got water in my eyes."

"Of course you can, baby girl." He held out his arms for her, and she swam right in, jabbering ninety to nothing about absolutely nothing at all.

Trey rested his chin on her head and let her talk.

Ap watched her, wide-eyed, then stared at him, making him grin.

Yeah, she could chat. Mostly, keeping up with her was nodding and smiling. She just wanted someone to hear her go on.

Amelia was swimming laps, back and forth, and Braden was… was he flirting with a girl?

Trey looked at Ap. He wasn't ready to do this again.

"What?" Ap looked around. "Oh. What should I do?"

"Nothing. They grow whether or not we want them to."

"Oh."

"Is it bad that Braden likes girls, Uncle Daddy?" Courtney asked.

"No, baby girl. People like who they like."

"Oh, okay." She nodded happily. "Do you like Uncle Ap?"

"I do."

Ames appeared between them. "Seriously? Like, like like?"

"Maybe." He winked at Ames, because he wasn't ashamed.

"If you like him, will he come home forever?"

Oh. Oh damn.

"Now, Amelia, you know I got to work." Ap said it easily.

"Right. Still…. We miss you when you're gone."

"I miss you guys too. So much."

"Who keeps you company while you're gone?"

Ap's smile faded. "I'm mostly on my own, kiddo."

"I'll come with you. I'm going to be a barrel racer." Bella leaned on Ap's feet. "Uncle Daddy won't mind."

"He might mind a little if you missed school." Ap stroked her hair.

"I might mind a little because I would miss my cowgirl."

Bella looked at him, lip quirking. "Yeah?"

"Yes, ma'am."

"I like the yaks." She said it like I love you.

"I love you too, Bella. Go swim."

She pushed away, slicing through the water like the athlete she was. Like her uncle.

He smiled as the other girls chased their sister. God, they were getting big. He was so proud of them he could bust. They made him happy.

"You're a good dad."

He shrugged. "I try to be. I try to make Tammy and Dan proud."

"You do." Ap looked at him, serious as a heart attack. "You really do."

"I hope so." He reached over to squeeze Ap's hand, real quick.

Ap's cheeks went red, but he just laughed, turning their hands to join their fingers together. "Feeling good in your bones now?"

"I am. I needed a soak."

"I didn't even know I did. I was a little sore." Oh, look at that laughing face.

"Just a little?" Next time he'd try harder.

"A twinge now and then." Ap rubbed the back of his hand with a thumb, making him breathe harder, making him glad he was in the water and not out on dry land in front of God and everybody.

"I bet you slept good, after."

"Oh hell yeah." Ap nodded slowly. "Like a baby."

"Me too. I look forward to tonight."

"Yeah?" Now Ap licked his lips, his eyes hot on Trey's face.

"Uh-huh. I'm all in for… whatever."

"Uncles! Watch!" Braden did a slow backflip in the pool.

They both laughed and applauded.

"Can you do it too, Uncle?"

"I bet Uncle Ap can," Trey offered.

"Lord." Ap moved out closer to the middle of the pool, then pushed backward, up into a handstand, then back down again.

He applauded as Ap came up, making a little hullabaloo for the man.

Ap bowed. "Thank you. Thank you."

Then Ap grabbed Courtney and said, "You ready to go under?"

She pinched her nose shut and squeezed her eyes closed. They went down, Ap holding his baby girl good and tight.

Trey was impressed. Court was very worried about her face being in the water. They popped up, Court squealing. "Again!"

"You ready, baby girl?" Ap asked.

"Watch me, Uncle Daddy! Watch me!"

"I'm watching!"

She scrunched up her face, then held her nose. Ap took her under, and boom, she was laughing again when he brought her up.

Ames sat next to him, quiet and close.

"Where you at, girl?"

"Huh?" She blinked at him, kinda dozy. "Can I take guitar lessons?"

Well, she rarely asked for anything, so he nodded. "Sure. Let's find you a teacher."

"Cool. This is really neat, Uncle Daddy. Braden looks so cute." She leaned against him.

"I'm glad you're having fun, Ames. We needed a good day off, didn't we?"

"We did. I want a hamburger with just a little green chile."

"Is there anything better than that for lunch?"

"Not for me!" She laughed.

"My girl." He hugged her close, knowing Bella would be the last one to wind down. He would have to keep an eye out.

"Yep. All yours."

She giggled, but before long she was sound asleep against his side.

Ap floated over, shaking his head. "She's out, huh?"

"Not before she requested green chile burgers."

"We'll round it up soon. Court is drooping, and my belly is growling."

"You'll have to get the Killer B's—they're in a pod over there."

"I'm on it."

Trey was really hoping the being good for Uncle Ap would carry through when Ap told them it was time to go.

He hoped they'd had enough fun to carry him through.

Braden and Bella looked over at him, where Court had joined him and Ames. To his ever-loving surprise, they both nodded at Ap, then started to wade to Trey.

"You ready for food?"

"I'm starving!" Bella proclaimed.

"Eee! I know, huh? I'm all hungry." Braden winked at him.

"Then it's time for Dave's Burgers!" He clapped his hands, making Amelia snort and sit up. Dave's was on the pueblo, and it was cheap, yummy, and filling.

"Taco burger!" Bella bounced out as Braden shook his head.

"Indian taco!"

"Green chile!" That was his girl.

Court, though, looked to Ap. "What are you having?"

"Maybe a Frito pie." Ap rubbed his flat belly. "I love those."

"I love a Frito pie! Uncle Daddy, can I have a Frito pie?"

"Sure, baby." Like she'd eat that. He hid his grin, though. He would get her fry bread or a corn dog, and she could try Ap's pie.

"I'm going to get Fritos with you, Uncle Ap."

"Sure, baby girl." Ap raised an eyebrow at him, and he tried not to snort. "Okay, everyone has to wash up, and real undies, not bathing suits under clothes, okay?"

Right on. Apparently yeast infections were a thing with little girls. An awful, terrible thing.

He didn't even want to think about it.

"Bella went without us!" Courtney was a little tired.

"I'll walk you to the door, and you can find Bella. Tell her I told her to stay with you." Trey walked the girl over to the ladies' locker room.

"Bella! Bella, you left us!"

"Come on, Courtney. We'll find her. Uncles will be right here." Ames shot him a look. "Right?"

"You know it." He would wait for them and trade off with Ap to go rinse off.

"God, another… how many years until we don't worry?"

"Eighty? Eighty-five, tops."

"Damn." Ap shook his head, peering after Braden, who was pretty confident. "That's crazy."

"Yeah. I think the boys are easier. My girls?" Not so much.

"They're amazing." Ap looked a little stricken. "God, you used to have to take them to the men's room."

"Up until two years ago, yeah." He'd had Cole scope out men's rooms for a while.

"You are a brave man, honey." Ap clapped him on the back.

"I'm Uncle Daddy, right?" Hell, if he looked at his situation full-on, ever, he'd panic, so he never looked. Ever.

"You are." Ap winked. "Do we trade off, or do we both need to stay here?"

"Go on. I'll wait until you're done."

"You sure? I don't mind." Ap touched his hand again, just a tiny show of affection.

"I'm good. So far, no one's screamed."

"Is that normal?"

"You've seen what happens with a simple spider."

Ap nodded, backing away slowly. "I'll check on Braden."

He chuckled softly. Yeah, the tough rodeo man had nothing on a women's bathroom. Hell, he was going to have to walk three little girls through their first periods. He was a motherfucking *stud*.

Bella peeked out the door. "Uncle Daddy, can you get the extra bag from the car? Courtney put on her clean undies and peed."

"I got it right here, kiddo. I brought it in."

"You rock. I told her I'd tell you she forgot."

"I've got your back, Sister."

"Thanks, Uncle Daddy." She grabbed the bag, and off she went. She and Cole and Braden had taken on so much over the years.

Of course, the little ones would too, as they grew up.

He grinned at himself. That would be a relief and a sadness all at once. He shook himself. Shit, he had eleven years before the last one left high school, and he'd be a grampa by then, he'd bet.

Ap joined him again, fully dressed. "Go on, honey. Braden is being slow."

"Ah, teenagers. Yay." He headed into the dressing room and got rinsed off, singing at the top of his lungs. That would get Braden moving.

"Uncle Daddy! So embarrassing." Braden strolled out of a stall. "You're still all wet."

"Yeah, I was watching at the girls' bathroom." He dried off. "Have fun?"

"For real. It was so good."

"Cool. Looks like you made some friends, huh?"

"Yeah." He ducked his head a little. "Is it okay if I message with Lily once in a while?"

"Lily? That's a pretty name. Sure. I don't see why not, so long as it won't get her in trouble." Lord have mercy. His boys.

"Nah. Her big brother said it would be okay. He's nineteen."

"There you go." *Damn, Sam.* "You ready to go eat?"

"I'm starving!" Braden patted his belly.

"I can tell. You're wasting away."

"Yep. I'm abused."

He nodded. "Beaten."

"Horribly." Braden laughed. "Go change. I'll help Uncle Ap."

"I'm almost ready. I'll be out in a sec."

"Okay." Braden left him, and he shook his head. Hamburger time.

Hell yeah.

Chapter Twelve

AP stared at the pecan pie where it sat on the oven rack. "It's still liquid."

"So cook it longer." Trey didn't seem worried. Why wasn't he worried?

Ap stared some more. "It's been in there an hour."

"We're high altitude."

"Yeah, but…."

"Ap, you do this every year. Give it time." Did Trey just touch his butt?

He blinked, then closed the oven. A few weeks of domestic bliss made the guy bold.

Ap was home at Thanksgiving every year. The first year after the crash had been brutal—Cole and Braden had been heartbroken, Bella had been completely confused, and the two little ones were terrified of him.

Trey had been in a panic, trying to recreate something that was close to Thanksgiving.

They'd ended up buying their feast from Walmart a day before, because the turkey had still been frozen and the pumpkin pie had sort of... fallen in on itself like a bad soufflé.

Six years they'd been doing this together. Six years of turkeys and hams, of friends and neighbors stopping by, of tears and laughter and the parade.

This was when Ap really felt as if he had a place here. A home.

"Uncle Ap? Can I help?" Amelia stepped close. "The boys are playing video games, and Bella and Court are playing with the dogs."

"Sure. I need someone to help put stuff on the relish tray." They liked to have nibbles, so he pulled out pickles and olives, cheese and veggies.

"Do I get to make it pretty?" She climbed up to the table, all smiles.

"You do. Here's ranch dip too. Careful, huh?" No one needed to lose a finger.

"I will. I promise." She started arranging veg, little face so focused.

He chuckled, then went back to chopping onions and celery for dressing. He would sweat them while Trey got the stale bread and cornbread ready.

Every so often he looked over at Trey, admiring the man's broad shoulders, that tiny butt. For such a big guy, Trey moved with an economy of motion Ap associated with athletes. Like bulldoggers.

"Uncle Daddy? Can me and Court go see the yaks?" Bella was filthy, completely covered in dust.

"Yes. Take the corgis." Trey went all stern. "Be careful, and don't spook anyone."

"I'll be good. I promise." Bella looked guilty, all the time.

"I know you will, kiddo. I just have to say it. Wear your boots."

Ap nodded. No one needed tetanus. "Watch your baby sister too."

"Oh, very nice," Trey murmured.

"Come on, Court!" The girls ran off.

Trey stepped to the kitchen doorway. "Can you guys set a timer to check on your sisters in twenty, please?"

"Sure." Cole didn't sound put out, so Ap guessed that was a good compromise. The boys would do dishes later.

Amelia was organizing vegetables by color, so carefully. His little chef. She made lines of the veggies on the big turkey tray he'd given her; they had a neighbor who gave them a new turkey platter every year.

"Good job, Ames. I'll take a picture when you're done."

"Will you put it on Instagram?"

"You'll break the internet."

Oh, that pleased her, didn't it? Deep down. She gave him a happy little grin before going back to putting together her puzzle.

Trey bumped hips with him. "I'll take over dressing if you baste."

"You got it." They had double wall ovens, so the pies could be in one while the turkey roasted in another. He basted that bird with its own juices, then checked the pies. "It's cooking!"

"Surprise, surprise."

He was going to swat Trey. Maybe pinch him.

Maybe kiss him.

He wondered what Trey would do if he just turned around and kissed the man on the mouth. He glanced at Amelia before tugging Trey with him to the pantry. There. Compromise.

"Ap?"

He loved that little flash of confusion.

Ap took the kiss he wanted, deep and long, and Trey opened right up, grabbing his ass. He laughed for sheer joy. Now this was something to be grateful for.

The door opened, Cole standing there in the light. "Seriously? You're old."

"What?" Ap blinked. "We are so not old."

"Too old to be macking in the closet."

"Well, you guys never let us have time anywhere else." Trey rolled his eyes. "Nothing is burning, right?"

"Just your old-dude passion."

"I will kick your skinny ass." Ap pushed past Cole, still holding Trey's hand.

"Dude, I outweigh you by eighty pounds."

"Cole." Trey's voice had a little chill.

"Sorry." Cole gave him a not-quite-sheepish look.

He was going to watch that. He'd talk to Trey, get some advice. He didn't want to have to kick Cole's ass. Still, he needed to know if he laid down the law, Cole would fall in.

"It's okay, man. Can you make sure the girls aren't setting any fires before you go back to your game, please?"

"You got it." Cole headed outside.

Trey looked at him, shrugged. "He has to figure out where he fits, I guess."

"Yeah, and where I do. I don't blame him, but I'll need him to have my back."

"He will. He's really beginning to... be grown. The next bit is going to be hard, I bet."

"Well, I got your back." He goosed Trey's ass.

"Yeah? I like that. A lot."

"The pinch or the back-having?"

"Both."

Ap grinned, then turned to Amelia, who had finished her masterpiece. "That's amazing, hon."

Was that a… buffalo? Out of broccoli? Wow. She was going to sell art when she grew up.

"Thanks, Uncle Ap. Can I make cranberry goo now?"

"You totally can. Careful, okay?"

"Uncle Daddy will help with the sugar." She was so certain Trey was right there for her. And he was. "Do you remember when I couldn't do this? When I was too little?"

"I do. I remember when all you did was sleep." He winked at her when she squealed.

"Do you think Bella's lying about remembering our momma and daddy?"

"No." No, he knew Bella was old enough to remember some stuff. "I know you're sad that you don't remember more, but I think she knows some stuff."

"It's just not fair. Everyone but me and Court remember."

"Oh." He knelt down to hug her. "I can tell you stories to help."

"It's not the same. I don't remember them at all." She grabbed on to him, though, and held on tight.

"They loved you so much. We can sit and look at pictures, maybe? After the goo? I want to tell you." She was breaking his heart.

"Oh. Oh, I would like to." She brought her lips to his ear. "It makes Uncle Daddy sad sometimes."

"I bet it does. He lives here, right? He sees what they could have had every day." He said it softly before kissing her cheek. "Goo?"

"Goo!" She nodded, the storm clouds gone in a flash. "I need pineapple and whipped cream and cranberries and...."

When he looked up, he found Trey watching them, this misty smile on his face.

He winked over, letting Trey know it was all okay. It was all going to be okay. Trey nodded to him before moving past him to unload box after box of brown 'n serve rolls.

"How many can these kids eat?" Ap asked.

"Cole and Braden can eat a box each."

"Wow." That wasn't really fair, to be so shocked. He'd downed his share before he had to cut the carbs.

"You're just the diet guy."

"Shut up." His cheeks heated. Ap had gained five pounds already, just being home. On the road, they were all in the same boat.

"You look amazing. I've never seen anything finer in my life."

His cheeks went hotter than he could ever remember. "Thank you."

He'd had a lot of folks—male and female—admire him, but Trey meant it. Trey looked at him like he'd hung the moon or held the ladder for the guy who had.

"Uncle Ap. Sugar!"

"Right." *Got it. Thanksgiving.*

"She's going to have you running your ass off come Christmas baking."

"I can't wait." He would have to leave soon, but finals would be over in time for him to come back and bake with his babies.

Then he was going to be home for a few months, and it was going to rock. He'd made a plan. He was going to try to win a day at the finals, at least. Get his ten thousand dollars on. Then he would skip Fort Worth and Denver. Maybe even San Antonio. He could start with Austin or Houston.

He wanted to be able to help around the house, maybe take everyone to the beach for spring break this year.

Oh now, there was an idea. Galveston would be a hoot. He would love to see how the kids reacted to the kelp....

And with two of them, they'd be able to handle the kids. Hell, Cole and Braden would be basically handling themselves. He would tell Cole to ask his girl along too. They could rent a house....

"You're smiling, Uncle Ap. Is that good?"

"It is, Ames. Real good."

"Oh cool. Pour and I'll stir."

"I got you." He poured sugar, watching her face as she concentrated hard.

"Uncle Daddy! I hate Cole." Bella came stomping in like a thundercloud, Courtney slinking in after her, head down.

"Do you? Why's that?" Trey sounded only the barest bit curious.

"Because I made her stop walking the top rail of the ostrich fence," Cole said easily, coming in to grab a carrot off the relish plate.

"Ah. Well, you know you're not supposed to be up there, don't you?"

"It's so tall! Courtney bet me!"

"She bet you...." Trey rolled his eyes. "Time to come in and wash up. You two can help set the table."

Court nodded, moving to wash her hands, but Bella glared at everyone impartially.

"Did you really bet her?" Ap whispered.

"Uh-huh. I double-dog betted her."

"Oh man." No one could resist the double-dog dare. No cowgirl, anyway.

"Good Lord," Trey muttered. "I just need ten or twelve more kids."

"At least." Neither of them could even yell. They would have done it too. "Bella, stop grumping and wash up. We're gonna have a good day even if I have to put Xanax in your turkey."

"Yeah, yeah. If they didn't convince Uncle Daddy to do that at school, you won't either."

He pulled a Trey and stared her ass down. She grinned, then flounced to the sink. Score one for Uncle Ap.

"Very nice," Trey whispered.

"Drugs?"

"Not going to happen with my kids."

"She doesn't need drugs." Bella was so far from needing to be medicated. She was just stubborn.

"I know that. I told them to shove it up their asses."

"Good on you."

He checked on Amelia, who was carrying dishes to the table, tongue caught between her teeth.

"Bella, Court, help your sister." Man, he sounded like a dad.

Cole started pouring iced tea, and Braden appeared, going to the sink to wash his hands. "What can I do?"

"Serving spoons, please."

Trey pulled the pie out, then started wrestling the turkey out of the oven, the huge bird wobbling. Cole jumped in to avert disaster, all of them hooting and hollering like they'd roped a dinosaur or something.

Lord, look at them and their feast. Them and their family.

Ap stood back for just a moment to enjoy the scene.

Then Phineas streaked through the kitchen, leaping to try to reach the table, and they were back to normal chaos.

Christ, he had a lot to be thankful for. Always had, but now he knew.

That made it even harder to think about leaving.

AP was doing crunches.

Hundreds of them.

It was fascinating, at least at first, and Trey watched for a while before heading out to get some work done.

All those crunches meant it was time for Ap to leave. He hadn't said anything yet, but finals started in just over a week, and Ap would have to go a few days early and get on a few practice animals.

It was no big deal. It was what Ap did. He wasn't going to be a shit about it.

He hoped.

Trey would miss Ap in his bed. A lot.

Hell, Trey would miss having another adult to help around here, to help with bedtimes and homework and the running around. Ap had surprised him, really. He was firm but fair, and he was damn good with Bella, helping her be more responsible and less reckless. Ap was patient with Ames too, talking to her endlessly about her folks, teaching her all the stories. Hell, Trey hadn't heard some of those tales, and they made his heart hurt but happy, if that even made sense.

"Uncle Daddy, can I bring Julianne to supper?"

"Sure. We're having enchiladas, okay?"

"Sounds great. I just want her to come before—" Cole shrugged.

"Sure, son." Because Ap was special. He got it.

It hurt a little, but he totally got it.

"Cool." Cole grinned at him, but those eyes were sad. "You're gonna miss him bad, huh?"

"It's a couple of weeks, son. He'll be home after he wins the big purse." *God yes.*

"Yeah, and then he'll go again in January." Cole shook his head. "This stay seemed different somehow."

"It was. It was longer—he usually stays just for Thanksgiving week and the two weeks at Christmas." And they were sharing a bed, talking about sharing a life.

"I like having him around." Cole chuckled. "Less driving for me."

"Yeah, yeah. You'll have a couple busy weeks of that with all the Christmas things."

"Yeah." Cole grimaced. "Guess making extra money is out."

"You help me out, I'll help you out."

"You got it. Thanks for letting Julianne come over. I'll go call."

He nodded and got back to stuccoing the house, patching around the faucets and windows.

Ap appeared about ten minutes later, maybe, heavy jacket on his skinny-ass body. "Hey. You need some help?"

"Hey, stranger. I'm running late, but it's been warm, so…."

"Well, God knows I can stucco with the best of them."

"Rock on. Cole's bringing the girlfriend to supper. He wants her to meet you again."

"Okay. She seems like a nice kid." Ap grabbed another joint knife so he could patch cracks.

"She does. She really likes Cole. I've talked on birth control a lot. We don't need babies."

"Not now, no." Ap sounded horrified. "Later, sure."

"Much later. Like another fifteen years." Like Cole would wait that long.

"I know." Ap chuckled. "So, should I make green chile apple pie?"

Trey grinned. He'd been amazed to find out that Ap was kind of a closet chef. The man could cook.

"Can you make one with and one without? Braden and Court don't like the heat."

"I can." Ap slathered on stucco, then textured it.

"Thanks. I'm making enchiladas." *I'm going to miss you, man.*

"Oh yum." Ap stepped close enough to bump against him. "You know I got to go tomorrow."

"I know. You going to tell the kids tonight or just let me do it after school?"

"I'll tell them unless you think it will cause a problem." Ap frowned a little.

"Nah. There will be some tears, but that's pretty reasonable." He could deal with that.

"Sure. Okay." Now Ap gave him a sideways look. "You okay?"

"Sure." He felt his cheeks heat. "I'm already looking forward to you coming home."

"Me too." Now Ap softened, relief on his face. "I thought you were pissed."

"Nah, jealous a little. I'd give a lot to come with you."

"Oh damn. I wish I could take you." Ap grimaced. "No way now."

"No, no. We have Girl Scouts Christmas, we have midterms, we have choir performances and...."

"I'll be back by the caroling thing, right?"

"You told Bella and Braden you would be, so you'd better be." He wasn't covering for Ap for that.

"I know. I'm on it. Finals end the sixteenth, and it's not until the twentieth."

"Yeah. You'll be here for the 4-H party too. We're supposed to bring chips." God, Ap was going to think he was so boring.

"Chips I can do." Ap gave him a wide, evil smile. "Beer is out, right?"

"Shit, Marcela would love you forever."

"I know, but the kids would try to sneak."

Yeah, Ap had caught Cole trying to sneak out with a six-pack from the fridge the day after Thanksgiving. Like they weren't going to notice.

Cole hadn't liked cleaning out all the outbuildings one bit. "Oh, I think you taught Cole a lesson on that one."

"I sure hope so." Ap's eyes twinkled. "Just using what Mom and Dad used on me. Is that how it always is? Parenting the way your folks did until you learn what works?"

"Yeah. I just keep trying shit and making it work."

"You do great. I had no idea how many moving parts there were." Ap was a damn good stucco-er.

"Me either," Trey confessed. If he had, he'd never have been able to do this.

"That's probably good." Yeah, Ap got it now, didn't he? It made Trey feel less alone.

He grinned at Ap. "You looking forward to getting back to work?"

"I'm hoping to get a check." Ap's return smile was muted some.

"I just want you home again safe for Christmas. Speaking of, what do you want?"

"Huh?" Ap peered at him. "For what?"

"Christmas?" *Dork.*

"Oh!" Ap's expression cleared. "Uh…."

He laughed at Ap. Like Ap had never been asked what he wanted from Santa.

"I could use a new belt." Ap nodded as if that was that. "What about you?"

"I think I'll ask the kids for a wallet."

"Okay." Ap agreed easily. "How many do you have now?"

"Thirteen, fourteen?" He chuckled, the sound starting low and growing.

Ap hooted, slapping his arm, and soon they were just tearing it up, laughing so hard they could hardly stand.

Braden appeared like magic. "What are you doing? Is it fun? Can I help?"

"Sure, kiddo." He pulled out another joint knife, this one smaller. "We're patching cracks. Put a good dollop of goo over the hole, then scrape it down." He demonstrated. "You need to find the ones down low, since you're all young."

"I can do it!" Braden took to it like a duck to water, chattering away to them both.

Ap bumped hips with him, and he closed his eyes, trying to pretend Ap wasn't going away tomorrow.

He wasn't a child. He wasn't a teenager in love. He was a grown man who knew Ap was coming back. All he had to do was have some patience and trust.

For now, he just needed to keep the damn house from falling down around their ears.

Chapter Thirteen

"**AP!**" Dean Farber trotted over to clap him on the back. "How's it hanging, man?"

"Good. About to get on some practice bulls."

"You have a good time visiting your nieces and nephews?"

"I did. I'm heading back for Christmas as soon as I can."

Dean waggled an eyebrow at him. "Can you stay one day after?"

Yeah, no. Not a chance. He had a big, hot blond waiting for him, someone that had been waiting for him. He would have, once upon a time, but that was when he thought he never had another shot at Trey.

"No, man, sorry. How's it going with you?"

"Good. I mean, good." Poor Dean, he looked so confused.

"Yeah? You gonna get on a bull today?"

"Might as well, if I'm not going to get a ride anywhere else…."

"Sorry, buddy. I got a steady thing." He might as well be flat-out honest.

"No shit? Good for you!" Dean grinned at him, slapped him on the shoulder. "I'll be damned."

"I know!" He didn't want to go into it too much. It was not new, but it wasn't old news either.

"I'll buy you a beer later. To congratulate you."

"Thanks, man. So who's the frontrunner in roughstock?"

"J398. He's a solid ride, not mean, but a good challenge."

"Yeah? Good deal. I'm hoping for Texas Tornado for my first pull on the broncs. She kicks damn fine." He always talked names, while Dean always did numbers.

"She'll get you some good numbers, that's for sure."

"That's what I need." He grinned sheepishly. "I really want a good Christmas for the kids this year. I want to win a go-round."

"How many are there again? Three? Four?"

"Kids? Five. And Cole is almost old enough to not be around as much at the holidays, so I need to make it count."

"Man, it's not every guy that would take on their brother's kids."

"Trey is the one who's done all the work." Trey made him feel humble. Not small or anything, but humble.

"You work your ass off, though. That's got to be hard."

"I'm good. I mean, I try." He shook his head. "How's your momma? Is her hand healing?"

"You know it. It would be better if she'd actually rest it, you know?"

"I bet." His mom had always been that way. Cut her fingertip off making carne adovada? Superglue. It was like magic. Gross magic sometimes, but magic nonetheless.

"Yeah. Moms."

"I miss mine every day." He whacked Dean's arm. "Let's go check out the stock for today."

"Works for me, cowboy."

The thing to focus on between now and the end of a week and a half of rodeo shows was sitting up, not getting down in the well, and riding his best. Then he could go home and have his holiday with his kids and his lover.

Oh, he did love the sound of that.

Chapter Fourteen

"**UNCLE** Daddy! My jeans tore!" Courtney came running up, holding her backside.

"How on earth…?"

"I did the splits! My pants didn't."

"Why were you doing the splits in jeans?" He was trying not to laugh. "You have special pants for gymnastics."

"I was showing Braden!" Like that was perfectly logical.

"Well, let me see." He needed to know if the jeans were salvageable.

She turned around and bent over, the seat split right down the middle.

"Whoops. Okay, go change." Hopefully, she wasn't attached to this pair and it could disappear. "Hurry now, we have to pick Amelia and Bella up."

"Okay!" Court pattered off, holding her butt again. As soon as she was out of earshot, he laughed hard. Good Lord and butter, they kept him on his toes.

"Uncle Daddy, do I have to come?" Braden popped up, damn near scaring him to death.

"Uh, I guess not. You sure you don't want to?"

"I want to get my homework done so I can watch movies tonight."

"Okay."

"Thanks. Tacos tonight?"

He nodded. He could do that. He'd pick some up in town.

"Thanks, Uncle Daddy."

"Anytime. Tell Cole when he gets home to stay, okay? Court? Come on!"

"Sure." Braden sounded so cheerful that Trey had to figure Cole had plans. Too bad he hadn't cleared them with Trey.

His oldest was feeling his wild oats these days, chafing at having to help out so much. Ap being there had spoiled them all more than a little. If Bella asked why he never did *x*, *y*, or *z* like Ap one more time....

"Court? Are you ready?"

"I am!" She ran out wearing a tutu and a coconut bra from Halloween.

Fuck.

"It's cold for the coconuts, Court. A shirt? Please?"

"Uncle Daddy!" She wailed it, and he clenched his teeth and counted to ten.

"Now."

"Uncle Ap let me wear it!"

"It was Halloween." He crossed his arms over his chest and stared. No more words. He hadn't lasted this long as a parent by giving in.

"Okay. I'll get a shirt." She could pout with the best of them.

"Fast." He didn't want to leave Ames standing out in the cold. Could be Ap leaving, but she'd been sniffly for a day or two.

He didn't need them all sick.

She came drooping back out wearing her rainbow unicorn shirt, which was nice and thick. "Good deal. Come on."

"I'm coming! I'm not bad!"

"I know that, kiddo. I just don't want Amelia to catch a cold. I told Braden we could have tacos." Lord, she was in a mood and a half.

"Can I have chicken?"

"Sure." He scooped her up and nuzzled her; his stubble was long enough after a few days of not shaving that it would tickle and not burn.

Courtney squealed and wiggled, but then she threw her arms around his neck. "I hate when it's cold and we can't play outside."

"I know, right? It stinks to be cooped up. Maybe this summer we'll build a play casita, just for you and Ames."

"Yeah?" She gave him big eyes when he carried her out to the van. "Oh! I can help with the adobe!"

He chuckled at how she automatically assumed it would look like the house. "No Victorian cottage?"

"That would get hot in the summer and cold in the winter," she scoffed.

"That's my desert baby." He helped her into the van, and she buckled herself in.

"Where else would I be?"

He laughed, heading out to pick up the middle sprogs. There was a lot of driving involved in kids. He whistled along with the *Moana* soundtrack as he drove, and Courtney sang loud. She did love that song by the Rock.

His phone rang and he hit the hands-free. "'Lo?"

"Hey, you." *Oh. Ap.*

"Hey, stranger. How were the practice bulls?"

"Uncle Ap!" Courtney squealed. "We're going to make a casita for me and Amelia!"

"Looks like we got our work cut out, kiddo. You two on the road?"

"We're picking up Amelia and Bella from dance class! Oh, Uncle Ap, we miss you."

Courtney had that right.

"I miss you guys too. So much." Ap didn't sound… down, exactly. More homesick.

"How's Vegas? Send pictures, huh?" He wanted to go. He wanted to go and see… anything.

"I will. I've got an autograph signing today, of all things. My sponsor sprung it on me this morning. The practice bulls were good. I ate at the biggest buffet last night, Court. They had lobster."

"Losbers? Were they yummy? Did they taste like bugs? Bella says that they told her in school they were just big bugs."

"Not one bit. They taste like really sweet trout."

Go Ap for picking a fish Court liked.

"Uncle Daddy, can you make me losbers?"

"Uh… maybe?" What did he know about that?

"I can do a big boil when I get home, honey. I talked all about it to the chef."

"Did you hear? Uncle Ap's making me losbers!"

"I did! How lucky!" Magical Uncle Ap.

"When are you coming home, Uncle Ap?"

"A week and a half or so, kiddo. I'll call later tonight, Trey?"

"Sure, Ap. We can chat."

"Cool. I love you guys so."

"Love you, Uncle Ap!"

"Love you, man. I'll talk at you tonight."

Courtney waited until Ap hung up. "Are you gonna marry Uncle Ap?"

Like Ap would marry a man. "Why do you ask, honey?"

"Because you sleep in the same room and he kisses you and he says I love you. Cole says Mom and Dad did that." So serious.

"Well, we'll have to see. Right now, we're just…." *What? Dating? Fucking?* What were they doing?

"Okay!" She turned up the radio to shout about how she was Moana, so he let it go.

He had kids to pick up and tacos to fetch.

Chapter Fifteen

AP bounced from foot to foot, warming up. God, he wanted to talk to Trey before he rode today, but it was too late, really. He was up for bareback broncs in ten.

He grabbed the top rail and squatted, feeling it in his quads and glutes.

The noise from the crowd and the buzz of the announcer were actually comforting, if he was honest. This was his world and had been since he was old enough to get his card. He could smell manure, popcorn, and beer.

Jorge Martinez warmed up alongside him. "You feeling lucky, Ap?"

"I'm feeling determined, man. How about you?"

"Ready to ride this bitch into the ground."

Yeah, assuming Jorge remembered to mark out. The man was disqualified more often for that.

He grinned, rolling his head back and forth on his neck. The big gray mare was stamping and pushing at the gate already, promising to be a ride and a half. He loved this old lady; she'd been horse of the year twice. She could be his ticket to big money, and if she wasn't, he had saddle broncs and bulls this week.

Whatever it was, he needed one to hit and hit big so he could hang with his family for a few months.

He took a deep breath. Okay, his rigging was on her. All he had to do was tie in and not get bucked off. Bareback was harder on the body than saddle bronc, but Ap found it easier to stay aboard.

Ap always felt pressure, but this time? Christ, this time he needed these rides. They were the ability to go home.

He blew out his breath, then nodded to Oscar, who was pulling gate. Time to climb on. He didn't have to be as careful to let the mare know he was coming as he did with a bull, but he did talk to her, watching her ears swivel.

"Up and down, right, lady? Let's do this."

She snorted, bobbing her head, and he knew she was ready. He gripped his rigging, raised his free arm, and rested his spurs above her shoulders.

The eight seconds went like owl shit, the mare bucking like that was what she was born for. He held on, confident he had marked out, and waited for the buzzer while he spurred and grunted.

The buzzer went, James was right there to grab him, and it was over. He grabbed that safetyman by the waist, dropped to the ground, and ran a few steps to keep his equilibrium. Then he found the mare's circle and ran the other way. He climbed the fence and looked to the scoreboard.

He heard the announcer the same time as he saw the board. "Eighty-three points, folks! That might win the round!"

Fuck yeah!

He pumped his arm, then took his rope and ran for the back to text Trey.

His phone was in his bag back in the locker room. *Eighty-three!* he texted.

It took a few minutes, but the answer buzzed back: *Rock on!*

Man, he wanted to just go to the truck and call Trey, but he needed to hang out and see if he was getting a check. Three more riders after him.

He just needed one to fall short or not mark out—thank you, Jorge—to make a check. Now, if he could win the whole go-round that would be better than second or third….

The next two riders hit around seventy, and he watched his name, sitting there at the top of the leaderboard. Herme would have to get an eighty-two to topple him. He loved the little Cajun to death, but Ap prayed he came in under eighty.

This was his time, goddamn it. His.

His heart pounded, sweat beading up under his hat. "Come on, come on!"

Herme made the eight, and he stared, willing his name to stay on the top.

"Herme Bonchamps with an eighty-one point five."

"Hell yeah!" He pumped his fist, then waved his hat in the air when he was announced as the round winner. He was gonna get a victory lap.

He couldn't wait to tell the kids. Bella would be so excited.

He texted Trey again, just to let him know he had to take his lap and get his check.

He damn near fell over when he did get his check— twenty-six thousand dollars.

Fuck yes. Yes! That was enough to take a few months off, for sure.

He wanted to dance, so he shook it on the way out to his truck. Boom.

He called the house, hearing, "… beat you until you cannot breathe, do you understand me?" when Trey answered.

Uh-oh.

"Who's gonna die?"

"Tonight? Braden. I think they've decided to take turns. He chose not to do his homework yesterday and forged my name on the paperwork."

"Oh shit. Well, I don't blame you if you beat him."

"Yeah. Hold on." There was a breath, then, "Amelia, bath. Courtney, get into bed. Bella, read your chapters. Braden? You sit there at the table and start copying pages for being a shit. Cole…."

"Cole's at work," Bella piped up.

"Right. Sorry. Tell me everything."

"Cole got a job?" When had that happened? They could go into it later. "I won the go-round in bareback today. I got the check, baby."

"Fucking A." Trey whooped, the sound happy and proud. "Oh, good on you. What was your score that took it?"

"Eighty-three. Closest was an eighty-one. I knew that mare would make me money."

"You did good. Lord, Ap. I bet you're on top of the world."

"I'm feeling pretty good." He couldn't stop grinning. "I mean, I could win every go-round and not catch up with Tremblay or Carter, but this was damn fine."

"Are you going to go do something fun?"

"Hell yes. I'm gonna come home early. If I don't make any more money, I won't stay for the short go, because I don't stand a chance. I have saddle bronc tomorrow and bulls the day after that."

"I wouldn't say no to that."

"Good." He climbed into the truck. He had a discount hotel this time around, because sleeping in his truck in downtown Vegas was downright dangerous, and there were no close KOAs where he could pitch a tent. Maybe he would order a pizza. "I miss you."

"I miss your face. Seriously. I didn't know how much until you left."

"Well, you got spoiled like I did." Ap laughed, the sound low and happy. Intimate.

"We all did." Trey sighed softly. "One day I'll come out and see."

"You will." He would love that, for Trey to see what he was good at.

"I want to talk to Uncle Ap, please? I read my chapter."

"Do you have time to talk to Bella?"

"Sure. I'm just heading back to the hotel."

"Uncle Ap! Uncle Ap, when are you coming home? We need you to be at the parties."

"I promise I will be there in time for parties, baby girl." He hooked into the speaker so he could be hands-free before starting out of the parking lot. "I love to take my hijos around and show them off."

"All the animals are good. The ostrich bit Uncle Daddy and tore up his shoulder."

"Oh, did he? When was Uncle Daddy gonna tell me that?"

"He only told us 'cause Cole had to superglue it shut."

"Oh. Ew." He chuckled to make her laugh with him, but God knew he'd done that more than once. "I love you, baby girl. Can I talk to Uncle Daddy again?"

"Uh-huh. I love you. Uncle Daddy! He wants to talk to you!"

"Thanks, kiddo. I'm fine, you know."

"Superglue?"

"Yep. Works like a charm." Trey sounded so nonchalant.

"You didn't mention it."

That got him a laugh. "If I told you every time someone around here got hurt, that would be all we ever spoke about."

"Well, I know that, baby. I just worry." It wasn't a new thing for him to worry about Trey, but it did seem… way more specific now.

"Thanks. I'm just a little tender now. That old bitch is mean."

"She is. We should sell her, Trey. She's just costing you output with no gain."

"Talk to Cole. They're his."

"Oh." He had a vague memory of Courtney telling him that Cole sold the eggs, but that was it. "Well, then he needs to take care of her, baby."

"Logic. Tell me about Vegas."

He had never realized how hungry Trey was for experience. "Have I sent pictures yet?"

"A couple. It doesn't look real. It looks like a television set."

"It kinda feels that way. Vegas is always sparkle on top and grit beneath." It wasn't his favorite city, but the hotels were cheap off strip, and food was plentiful.

"Huh. Sort of like here, without the sparkle."

He chuckled. "Bernalillo has more neon these days. Think of the Denny's, man."

"Mmm… grits. I may have to take the kids on Saturday."

"You can get grits here, can you believe it? The Excalibur buffet."

"Crazy. Is that the one shaped like a castle?" Trey sounded a little wistful.

"It used to be way more kitschy, but everything is about classy kinda now." All those new hotels, dripping with crystals and thirty-dollar waffles.

"Ah. I'll stick to the casino. There's always the Tamaya if I want to get my fancy on."

"Yeah. That's where you went, right? When you had your time off?" He still wondered what Trey had gotten up to.

"Yeah. I ordered a lot of room service and drank beer in the bathtub."

"Oh, decadent." He chuckled. He got that. Ap figured he was taken now. He would do a lot of hotel stuff alone.

"Yeah." Trey's voice got soft, low. "It would have been all decadent if you'd been there."

"Oh, now." That gave him thoughts. "We really need to make more friends who could babysit the kids overnight."

"Yeah, wouldn't that be something?"

His whole body tightened. "Yes, it would. We might be able to convince Cole and Julianne to do it for enough cash."

"I could handle that. You and me, dinner in the room."

"A big bathtub for two." Uh-huh. He was so texting Cole tonight and bribing him.

"Mmm. I never did that before…."

"Me either. I showered with a couple of guys once, but that was water conservation. Nothing sexy about it." Some campgrounds charged extra for showers. A lot extra.

"Yeah, but this would be… on purpose."

"It would. I have an agenda here." He was gonna drive off the road, he wasn't careful.

Trey's chuckle sent peace right into him. He liked that, knowing he'd made it better.

"Uncle Daddy! Help me!" He could hear Amelia bellowing, sounding pretty pissed.

"Okay. I'm coming. Can I call you later? From my cell?"

"Yes. Please." He wanted to just talk until he fell asleep, like they'd done at home.

"Good deal. Let me deal with homework and getting hooligans to bed, then I'll call."

"I'll be waiting." That would give him time to call for a pizza. He grinned wide. Even life on the road was better with a lover to share it with.

Chapter Sixteen

GOD, Trey's head was going to pop right off. Honestly, it didn't seem like such a bad idea. If he didn't have a head, he wouldn't have ears, and he wouldn't have to listen to the constant noise.

Cole was complaining about having to balance his new job at Denny's with school and taxiing his siblings when Trey couldn't. Braden was pissed about his science project, Amelia was asking to go somewhere, Court was crying, and God knew where the fuck Bella was.

Probably setting something on fire. He rolled his eyes.

"Cole, I'm sorry, but I have to meet the farrier in ten minutes to work on Bettie's foot. I told you that yesterday."

"I have to be at work. She can miss one guitar lesson, or she can sit and wait for her teacher outside."

"Don't make me miss, Uncle Daddy! Please! I'll be good!"

"It's snowing. I'm already stressed out enough with you driving yourself…."

Cole rolled his eyes. "Please. I'm fine."

"I can worry if I want to. Can you wait for teacher outside, Ames? You have to bundle up good." He hated it, but it was the only solution at hand.

"Uh-huh. You'll come pick me up, right? You won't forget me."

"Have I ever forgotten you?" *Silly girl.*

"No." Look at that smile. "I'll wear all my winter stuff."

"Be nice to her, huh?" he told Cole, pulling on his gloves. It was cold as a witch's tit out there.

"I am. I can't wait for Uncle Ap to get home."

"Yeah." Him too. "Braden, watch your sister."

"Which one?"

"Boy, don't start. You're the one that switched out your feeding duties with Bella. You get to watch Courtney."

"She can watch TV." Braden got all mutinous.

"Braden Allen!" He was just about done.

"Amelia! Come on!" Cole hollered.

"Coming!"

"Don't yell at me!"

He turned on Braden, his temper sizzling up along his spine. He took a deep breath, forcing himself to sound calm, even when he wanted to shake the little shit hard. "Give me your tablet and go to your room. Now."

"But—"

"Now."

"Yessir." Braden thrust the tablet at him, scowling.

"Amelia, now. Courtney, get your boots and coat. You're coming with me."

"Okay, Uncle Daddy! Can I bring my baby doll?"

"Sure, honey."

She was the fastest of all the kids to get boots and a coat, and she put her baby doll in a fuzzy blanket to bring her along. He got Cole and Amelia gone before taking Court down to the barn.

"Bella? You out here, girl?"

There was no answer, and Trey frowned. She wasn't one to tease and play hide-and-go-seek.

"Bella?" He opened the barn door. "Baby girl? You here?"

Courtney went running down the aisle, skipping and calling to the horses. "Hey, Copper, hey, Rhoda. Hey, Marky. Hey…." She stopped short, her baby eyes going wide. "*Uncle Daddy! Uncle Daddy, help!*"

He didn't think, didn't breathe.

He ran.

Trey skidded to a halt, the sight of pink Ropers splayed wide and splashed with blood enough to tear him in half. "Bella? Courtney, get back. Bella, baby, I'm here."

He muscled his way into the stall, Bettie stamping and snorting. A hoof pick lay on the straw, blood on the tip.

Oh, sweet Jesus. He knelt at her side, afraid to touch her but knowing he had to. "Stay with me, Bella. I'm right here."

"Trey? You in here?" Gary Esposito came running into the barn, carrying Courtney, who was crying a little hysterically.

"Gary, man, call 911. Please. Please, call now."

Chapter Seventeen

AP stretched, pondering what he needed to do.

He'd gotten another check for fourth place on the saddle broncs. Six thousand dollars. Not too shabby. Today was bull riding, and that was the conundrum.

He'd pulled a bull named Rootin' Tootin', and he was a head buster. He'd sent three cowboys to the hospital this season alone. Ap was thinking of turning out, truth be told, and heading home.

Tugging out his phone, Ap tried to get his head in the game. He texted Trey: *Tell me to cowboy up and that it's only eight seconds.*

He waited a few minutes, then sent another text: *Tell me to ride, baby.*

When he got no answer, he checked the day sheet. Four more barrel racers. Ap ducked behind the chutes to dial Trey's cell phone. Trey always answered, even if he was in the truck.

It went straight to voicemail. Shit, Trey must be out of battery. Ap called the house. "Come on. Come on, now. I need your voice."

"Uncle Ap?" That was Ames. "Oh, are you at the hosp—"

"Amelia!" Cole grabbed the phone. "Hey. What's up?"

"What's wrong?" *Hospital?* That had to be what she was saying. Ap started toward the rider area. He was turning out right now.

"Uh. Are you okay?"

"I'm fine. I was trying to get Trey. He's not answering his cell."

"I... I'll tell him as soon as I see him." Cole was hiding something. Sixteen was a terrible time to start lying.

Ap *grrred* a little. "Son, you tell me what's wrong so I don't have to come beat it out of you."

"Uncle Daddy said not to worry you 'til after you rode."

"I'm not riding tonight." He found Sara, the lady working rider registration, kinda giving her hand signals to give him the sign-in sheet so he could withdraw. "What the hell is going on?"

"Bella's at Central. Bettie kicked her in the head. It's real bad. The ambulance came." Cole let the panic show. "I got all the others. I fed them. What do I do if he can't come home?"

"You're there alone with the kids?"

"Gary stayed with everyone and called me at work. I got Amelia and came home. Gary bought a bunch of pizzas and then headed down the hill to see how Bella is."

Okay, so the kids were all home but Bella, and they had food for at least a day. It was a nine-hour drive home. "Okay, kiddo, I'm leaving now. All you have to do is get everyone to bed, okay? Hell, if everyone is freaked-out, you can all sleep in the front room on the couches so no one is alone."

He wrote "family emergency" as his reason for pulling out of the go-round.

"I wasn't supposed to mess up your ride. Uncle Daddy said it was important."

"I made enough this week, son. I'm in the top ten, so I'll have my spot next year." He checked the box to forfeit his entry fee, and Sara gave him a one-armed hug. "I'll be there about five tomorrow morning."

"Yes, sir. Thank you. She's going to be okay, right?"

"She's gonna be fine. This is Bella. She's my cowgirl."

"Okay. I'll… I'll be here holding down the fort." Cole sighed. "Come home, Uncle. We need you."

"I'm on my way." He was too. He grabbed his gear bag and chaps, and he was on his way to his truck. "I love you, and my phone will be plugged in. You call me if you need anything at all."

"I will. I promise. Be careful."

"I will. Oh, does Bella have a room number?"

"Intensive care at the pediatric unit. They said PICU?"

"Okay, kiddo. You hang in there."

"Will do. I love you." Cole hung up the phone, and Ap took a couple slow, cleansing breaths.

Jesus. Bella was hurt, and Trey hadn't even—no. He had to focus on getting home. His suitcase was in the truck since he'd already decided this would be his last go-round. He needed to get the hell on the road.

They needed him at home.

TREY waited to call until midnight, needing to hear Ap's voice.

He sat in the PICU waiting room with his thousandth cup of coffee, his phone plugged into the wall.

"Hey, baby." Ap's voice filled the empty space around him.

"Ap." He fought his tears, fought to breathe. "Please. Come home."

"Hey. I'm on my way. I just stopped to pee in Williams so I could go on by Flagstaff. How's our girl?"

"It's bad. She's been in surgery. I need you. She's in a coma, and... I can't do this alone. Please." He wanted it to be him, not her.

"Shit. Oh, Jesus, Trey." Ap sounded... worried. Tired.

"I wanted to wait 'til you rode. I didn't want you getting hurt." He didn't want Ap to be distracted.

"I turned out, baby. I think I knew something was wrong, and you weren't answering, and I pulled Rootin' Tootin'."

"That bull's an evil bastard." Trey rubbed his forehead. "Cole's hanging in there. He's got everyone in bed."

"I called the house when you weren't answering. I know you were in the surgery area, baby. No stress. I kinda talked him down."

"Thank you. I'm... I hate this." He didn't know what to do. He'd had a kid in the hospital before, sure—but not like this.

"I'm sorry I'm not there. I have to go to the house first. Is, uh, Gary still with you?"

"No. He's the farrier. He was a huge help."

"Oh man. Was he coming to work on Bettie?"

"Yeah. Looks like that's what Bella was doing, working on Bettie's hoof. I told her to stay out of the stalls of the hurt ones. You've heard me. Over and over."

"She wants to be a hero so bad, baby." Ap chuckled, the sound tired more than amused. "I heard you, but did she?"

"You know she did. She just didn't care. She wants to grow up so fast." *And now.... No.* No, he was not even thinking that.

"They all do. Cole is holding it together. He said Braden wanted to sleep with the girls. Your farrier got them pizza."

"Yeah, he came by and sat with me during her surgery." They had to reduce the swelling, they said. Bruises on her brain, they said.

"I can't even imagine this, Trey. She's gonna be okay."

"Of course she is." He'd never forgive himself if she wasn't. He'd just lost track of her for what? Twenty minutes.

"I'll be at the house in four and a half, five hours. I'm making good time."

"Good deal. I'll be here until she wakes up or they make me leave."

"I'll bring you a bag of stuff when I come down, I promise."

"Okay. Thank you, Ap. I need you. I need you here." He was scared, so scared that he couldn't remember how to breathe.

"I swear. I'm coming home." Ap's voice was all determination.

"I'm so sorry." He let his head drop into his hands, sucking in desperate air.

"No. No, baby. This isn't your fault. Bella's just too damn strong for her own good. But that means she'll fight to heal." Ap just babbled for long minutes, letting him cry. His man-of-few-words cowboy had a lot of them when it came to this.

Finally the storm blew over, leaving him empty and shaking but ready to start again, to fight for his oldest girl to get back on the horse, so to speak.

"Hey. Better, baby?" Ap's voice held nothing but care, the words soft and gentle.

"Yeah. It's been a shit day, man."

"I bet. I'm so sorry you have to deal with all this. I'm coming."

Probably faster than he should, knowing Ap.

"You just be careful. You sleep if you need to." He needed Ap safe.

"I will." Ap chuckled low. "I slept until ten this morning. I swear, riding makes me lazy."

"Ten? Damn." He chuckled. "I think the critters would break the windows to have me feed and milk."

"The goats would explode. Can you catch a nap somewhere?"

"I'm in the waiting room while she's in ICU. When she has a room, I'll be able to sleep in the room with her."

"Okay. I'll pray for that soon. I'm doing a lot of praying."

"You and me both, honey." His phone started buzzing, and he sighed. "I'm going to answer texts. There will be tons of people offering to help and feed us, come morning."

God love the New Mexico Small Town Phone Tree.

"That's exceptional, baby. Okay, Flagstaff ahead. I love you. I'll see you this morning."

"I love you. Be careful." He hung up, closing his eyes just for a second. Just a minute. Just to make them stop hurting.

He could do this, and Bella would be herself again in no time. Ap was coming. He just had to make it there.

Chapter Eighteen

AP pulled into the drive at the ranch, and it looked like the kids were having a hell of a party. Cars and trucks were parked all over the dirt area they usually used for loading trailers and firewood. There was even a bicycle or two. *Wow.*

He parked at the back and hiked in, because he would have to run down to the hospital to spell Trey soon. First he needed to see his kids.

It was Amelia who found him first, his sensitive girl sobbing on the front porch. She looked up at him, pretty blue eyes watery and bloodshot. "Uncle Ap! You came back!"

She launched into his arms.

Ap hugged her to his chest, his own throat clogging up, his eyes stinging. "Hey, baby girl. I'm right here."

"You have to make it better. Everything is wrong. Please. Help me."

"I got you now. I'm gonna help as much as I can, okay? You need a Kleenex?"

"Uh-huh. My head hurts. Bad."

"I bet. All that crying. We'll get you a little Tylenol." He carried her into the house, knowing she was on the porch because of all the people in the kitchen. He smelled green and red chile, meat cooking, and fresh bread.

The Girl Scout leader was there, the football coach and half the team, Amelia's guitar teacher, their neighbors on both sides, and every abuelita in Bernalillo. *Wow.*

"Señor Ap!" A sweet old lady was holding a sleeping Courtney, rocking her gently. "My José and Ephraim are feeding and milking. Don't worry."

"Hi, uh, Dolores. Wow, it's been a while. Thanks so much for coming." The last time he'd seen her was the funeral. The funerals. They'd done everyone at once, and he'd about fallen over dead himself at the end.

"Of course. We take care of our own."

"Uncle Ap." Cole stood there, caught between being a boy and a man, but so much closer to a man right now than he had been two weeks ago. "You... you made it."

"I did, buddy. Ames, do you know where your Tylenol is?"

"I'll help her, sir." A kid about Cole's age held out his arms. "Come on, Ames."

Amelia went with him, so Ap gave Cole a bone-crushing hug. "Thank you, kiddo. You're amazing."

"I came home as soon as I heard. I picked up Amelia and came home." Cole shook for a second, then straightened up. "You tell me what you need me to do, Uncle. I'm on it."

"Right now, I need you here, sort of riding herd on all these people." He winked.

"Yes, sir. I'm on it. Uncle Daddy said we can stay home from school today. The animals are getting taken care of."

"They are. Dolores says her guys are doing it. Do we need anything? Food is covered, it looks like. Toilet paper? Paper towels?"

"We're dealing with that stuff, Ap." Coach Mike stood there with a smile. "We brought paper plates, cups, toilet paper, that sort of thing. I've spoken to the manager at Denny's too, explained that one of my players needed some time off, so his job will be safe."

"Thank you." He shook Mike's hand. "I can't tell you how much I appreciate it."

"We're a team, right?"

Cole nodded. "We are. Thank God."

"You know it." Mike smiled. "I've got to head into work. You have my number, Cole. Use it. Missy and me will be over tonight to spend the night so y'all can be at the hospital, Ap."

"Thank you." He was a little choked up at the goodness of their friends. Hell, he hadn't earned this friendship, but they were here nonetheless.

"Anytime." Mike clapped him on the arm, then headed out.

"Uncle, can you go talk to Braden? He won't come out of his bedroom."

"Sure, Cole." He patted Cole's back on the way by. Braden wasn't one to hide, so that sounded ominous. He knocked gently. "Braden? It's Uncle Ap."

The door opened a crack. "Hey."

"Hey. Can I come in?"

"Are you going to yell at me?"

"Why would I yell at you?" Ap didn't push the door, but man, he wanted to.

"Because this is all my fault. It was my day to feed, and I didn't want to."

"Oh, kiddo, this is not your fault." He pushed the door open, steering Braden through the clutter so they could sit on the bed. "She knows better than to try to doctor Bettie on her own. I bet she does it again anyway."

"I'm sorry. I'm so sorry she's hurt. Is she going to die because of me?"

"No. She's going to be okay." After years on the rodeo circuit, Ap knew what kind of miraculous recovery could be made with head injuries these days. She would fight hard.

She was young. She was strong. And he wouldn't accept anything less.

He hugged Braden to him. "I love you, okay?"

Braden leaned on him, sniffling, but Ap didn't comment on the tears. "Is Uncle Daddy mad at me?"

"I doubt it, bud. He may talk to you a bit about doing what he asks, but he's not mad." Poor kid was shaking.

"You swear?"

"I swear. Your uncles love you more than anything. I promise you."

"Okay." He wiped the back of his hand across his nose. "I need to wash up."

"You do. I'm gonna go check on the girls." He patted Braden on the back. "Come out when you're ready. There's food."

Tons of food. Vast amounts of food.

"I'm not hungry, but I could eat a sandwich."

"I bet Dolores will make you grilled cheese."

"Okay. I should come out and play with Ames and Court, huh? I bet they're scared."

"Amelia could totally use your company. Something kinda quiet. She's melted down."

"We can watch Nick Jr. It's for babies, so it's easy, and it'll make her laugh."

"Oh, that's a good idea. Just don't call her a baby." He winked when Braden glanced at him uncertainly, making Braden laugh.

"It's good, you being home. Uncle Daddy misses you."

"Does he? I miss him, and all you yahoos too." He did. God, he did.

"Me too." Braden gave him a hug, then backed off.

"Okay. You have your mission." He needed to pack a bag for Trey, check on the guys in the barn, and check on Bettie the horse, as well. Not to mention making sure someone was going to be here with the kids for the rest of the day.

There had to be someone. Coach was coming back with his wife, so someone just had to stay until then.

"You look wiped-out, Denny." The parish priest, Father Garcia, caught him in the hallway. "You ought to sleep before you drive downtown. It's so early."

He looked at his watch. It was just about seven thirty. "I caught a nap at a truck stop. That's why I'm a little late." Guilt had eaten at him, but if he died on the road, he was no help to anyone.

"How about I drive you down? I know Trey has a truck there. I'd like to be able to say a prayer for her."

"Oh." His eyes stung again. "I would really appreciate that, Father." If they had to coordinate another car, someone would come down.

"No problem. Let's grab a couple of tacos each, and we'll head out."

"I can totally have a taco." He stopped himself from saying murdering one, because you know, priest.

He needed to check on Court as well. She needed to see his face. "I'm going to grab Trey a bag. Can you send Courtney in to hug me if she's awake?"

"I can. I'll get those tacos in the kitchen too." Father Garcia left, and he headed to his and Trey's bedroom, where he grabbed a couple of days of clothes and toiletries.

He needed to get down there; he needed to see Bella with his own eyes.

"Uncle Ap?" Courtney's voice was very small and very sleepy.

"Hey, baby." He turned to hold out his arms for her. "Come here?"

"I seed Bella's blood. Her's hurt bad."

Lord, he hadn't heard baby talk from her in forever.

"She is. She had surgery, though, and they're watching her super careful." He picked her up and held her close. "I'm sorry you had to see that."

"Uncle Daddy cried." She snuggled into him.

"I bet. You can't blame him for that, right? It's scary for all of us."

He carried her and Trey's bag to the kitchen.

"Hey, Court." Cole was right there. "You want to come watch cartoons with Braden and Ames? There's blankets and pillows and color books and crayons."

She nodded. "Are you home, Uncle? All the way home?"

"I am, baby girl. I promise. I'm gonna go see Uncle Daddy, but I'll be back."

She hugged him again, holding him tight. "I love you. So bad. Tell Bella to come home and I'll share my baby doll with her."

"I will. I promise." He was making a lot of promises. She went with Cole, so he hoovered up two tacos. "Has anyone looked in on Bettie? The horse who kicked her? She was having hoof issues."

"Mr. Gary stayed and worked on her hooves, did the evening feeding and milking with Cole when he got back," a grizzled older man he didn't recognize told him.

"Ap McIntosh." He held out a hand.

"José Maez. I belong to Dolores. I'm the little adobe three ranches over."

"Nice to meet you." He shook hands. "Thank you and your family for all you're doing."

Father Garcia handed him one more taco. "Eat up, son."

"Yes, Father." God, this was heaven on earth, and hellish, all at the same time.

He ate up, then went to wave at the kids. They didn't need him pulling them away from each other. "Okay. I'm ready."

"Let's do this. I know Trey's waiting for you, and so's that little girl."

"Yessir." He was going to do this even though it terrified him. That was what parents did.

God help him.

TREY prayed for hours, and then he had another coffee and prayed some more. He prayed for Bella. He prayed for the kids at home. He prayed for Ap. He prayed for forgiveness.

Everything in his body hurt.

He sipped his coffee, wincing when yet another chirpy talk show came on. He heard someone come in, so he looked up, and damn if it wasn't Ap and Father Garcia.

He stood up, swaying a little bit, blinking to clear his eyes.

"Hey." Ap hurried to him, grasping his upper arms. "Hey. You're okay."

"You made it." He focused on Ap's green eyes. "She's still in a coma. There's a lot of swelling, but she's hanging in there."

"Hanging in there?" Ap searched his face in return.

"Her vitals are stable, and she's got brain activity."

"That's good, baby. Listen to me. I've seen this a thousand times. She's a cowboy. We come back from this."

He clenched his teeth against the cry that wanted out, but then he found a smile. "She is a cowboy, down to the bone."

"Yep. And she's young. Strong."

"Trey, would you mind if I went in to see her? They know me here." Father Garcia smiled gently at him.

"Please, Father. Tell God we need her here."

"I will." Father Garcia gave him a one-armed hug when Ap stepped back to give him room.

As soon as the good father was gone, Ap looked at him, not missing a thing. "Bathroom."

"This way." He dragged Ap down the hall, past the nurses' station.

Ap followed him, and as soon as they were sure they were alone in there, Ap was hugging him close and kissing him with a fierce desperation. He held on tight, sobbing into the kisses.

"I got you. I got you, baby." Ap cried with him, just holding him.

"I swear to God, I told her to be careful. I told her not to mess with Bettie."

"I know you did." Ap rocked them back and forth, almost like a dance. "She's so stubborn."

"She is. Her poor baby head, Ap. You…. God, the blood." He rested hard, knowing that he wasn't alone now.

"I told Courtney, and I'll tell you. I'm sorry you ever had to see that. Christ, baby. I'm here now." Ap just kept talking, which was what he needed.

"Thank God. How are the kids? Are they holding up?"

"They're scared. Braden thinks you're gonna blame him." Ap smiled a little. "I told him you might talk to him about doing what you ask him to, but that was it."

"It's been a hard week. I'm sorry you had to leave, but I'm so glad to have you here."

"No. I really was leaving. I was calling the house to tell you when Cole answered." Ap was serious as a heart attack. "Baby, why didn't you tell me?"

"I didn't want your mind here when you were sitting on the back of a bull."

"No, I get that. I do. But Rootin' Tootin' is just a bad bull, and something was telling me to get home."

"Yeah. We needed you." He needed help, needed a friend, needed his lover.

"I love you."

That was the second time Ap had said that in the last two days. God, he hoped it was true. Like really real.

"Good. I don't want to be the only one in this...." Trey's phone rang, and he grabbed it. "Yeah?"

"She's got a bleed. We've called the surgeon."

He grabbed Ap's hand and ran.

Chapter Nineteen

AP had never been so tired in his whole life. Then again, he didn't think he'd ever been as scared. Bella had come through the surgery, and they had her stabilized, but—

But damn, that was like her having a stroke.

They sat together, hands linked, neither one of them saying a thing.

Ap was afraid Bella wasn't the only one broken here. Trey's shoulders were hunched, the strong man's face lined with his fear.

He wanted to tell Trey it would be fine, that she would sail through this, but he didn't want to lie.

Hell, he was fighting puking with every fiber of his being.

"I don't know what to do," Trey whispered. "I've spent the last six fucking years not knowing what to do, and it's not getting better."

"Do you think Tammy and Daniel would know what to do right now? Or our folks? No one knows, baby."

"I keep waiting to be good at this whole thing with the kids. I keep waiting for it to be okay."

"Baby." He squeezed Trey's hand. "You are good at it. So good. I know you don't feel it now, but this isn't your fault." He squeezed, trying to get that through.

"I know. I mean, no more than anything. I just hate this. I swear to God, I'd take her place in a second."

"I would too. But neither of us needs to get hurt." He grinned a little, then glanced at Bella. They'd let them both come sit for a few hours because of the surgery. Soon they would probably have to go back to trading off, but that was damn lonely.

"Fair enough." Trey reached out and stroked Bella's cheek. "You need to get better, baby. You have yaks that need tending."

She didn't move, and she was so pale it hurt to look at her, but he touched her poor baby arm, full of needles and monitor thingees.

She was warm, and that helped. She was here with them, fighting to get better.

"Did you know that I have some friends from the finals coming down when you're better? A couple barrel racers want to meet the girl that's going to kick their asses."

Trey chuckled, the sound a little clogged. "We really need a casita."

"Someone told me you'd promised a little playhouse in the back."

"Oh yes. For Ames and Court."

"Uh-huh. We can make a little casita instead, with a bedroom and a front room. They can use it like a family room unless we have guests, huh?" He kept stroking Bella's arm.

"You know Bella will raise chickens in it."

Was that a smile? Could she hear them?

God, he hoped so. The doc said talking to her was important, that her brain activity would be increased by it.

"I bet she will. Maybe turkeys. Didn't she sneak quail babies in last year?"

Trey snorted. "Quail. She has a little setup for them in the back so the hawks can't get at the babies. Like we need more quail."

"She loves them; don't you, baby girl?" It felt so strange not to hear her laugh at them.

"She's our cowgirl, to the bone. She's going to work the ranch like a hellion. I'm so damn proud of her."

Trey's words were strong, fierce, and yes, that was a smile.

"She is. You are, baby girl. I can't wait to get you a barrel horse. I have a buddy who trains them. He's a horse whisperer like you're the yak whisperer." He babbled, wanting more reactions.

Trey looked at her, and he saw Trey's face relax at her smile. "Oh Lord, you do that and I bet she names it the Trigger. You know, I'm pulling the Trigger?"

"Oh God." Ap had to laugh, and if it was low and pained, so be it. "No. I bet she calls him Roland. You know, Roland the barrel?"

Trey laughed, and this one was real, almost shockingly loud.

Bella's fingers curled, and Ap grabbed her baby hand, letting her hold on. "You there, baby girl?"

She squeezed his hand.

Her eyes weren't open, and he knew the doctors would say she wasn't awake, but he knew better. She was right there. Oh God, she was there. Tears streamed down his face. "We see you, baby. We're right here. Me and Uncle Daddy."

"You know it. We're here, planning your life." Trey knocked their shoulders together. "We've decided to marry you off to a bulldogger named Ralph."

Her little face screwed up in a frown.

"Oh, see, I thought we'd decided on that boy from church. Esteban?"

"The boy that picks his nose? Nah, Braden wouldn't approve."

"Yeah, ew. Okay, Ralph it is."

She squeezed his hand again, and her monitors beeped a little faster.

"We'll build them a house across the street so we can see her whenever we want to." Trey's eyes were glistening, but that smile was real.

"I like it. No one leaves the ranch. Bum bum bum." He made ominous noises.

Her mouth moved, like she was trying to talk to them. Like she was dreaming.

Oh, thank God.

A nurse knocked softly before entering. "Hey. I saw her numbers go up. I just thought I'd check in."

"She's smiling and trying to talk."

"Yeah? That's great. Let me page the on-call and we'll have him give her a peek." She came over to the side of the bed and smiled. "I can't wait to talk to you, Bella. Did you know that's my daughter's name too? After the book. I loved *Twilight*."

"Her great-granny was an Isabella." Trey grinned when Ap looked at him, wide-eyed.

"Oh, that's great. How many do you have?"

"Five in total. We have two boys and three girls."

"Wow. That's so cool." She saw Bella's face move and made a happy noise. "Let me get the doc, huh?"

"Please." Trey leaned close. "I see you in there, baby girl. Uncle Ap is home, and we love you."

He loved them both so much he could hardly breathe. For the first time since Cole had told him about the injury, Ap thought it really might just be all right.

Trey squeezed his hand and rested against his side.

Yeah. They couldn't relax too much; she wasn't out of the woods yet. She was their girl, though, still in there and fighting.

Their cowgirl.

Chapter Twenty

TREY missed his house. He missed his bed. He missed his sons and his baby girls.

He wanted to sit at his kitchen table and drink his coffee and listen to his kids chat about school.

Instead, he was down in the waiting room, waiting for Bella's teacher to come out of the ward. They were back to one visitor at a time.

She was awake, though. Awake and in there. She was having a little trouble with walking and using her left hand, but the physical therapists were all enthusiastic and encouraging.

His phone rang again, and he glanced down. If it wasn't Ap, he didn't care. He loved that the community was with them, but he needed a second to be quiet.

Ap. He clicked Answer. "Hello?"

"Hey, baby. How's it going?"

"Miss Traynor's here visiting. I'm sucking coffee and Excedrin. How's you?"

"I'm ready to come trade off. The kids are gonna plotz if they don't see you soon."

"Yeah. She's wide-awake. She threw a temper tantrum today." It had made him so happy. She was on fire.

"I never thought I'd be glad to hear it. Amelia wants to play her solo for you, and Cole wants to talk about Christmas."

The unspoken question was right there—was Bella going to be home by then?

"Sure. God. I hate this…." He wanted to go home. He wanted to bring Bella home.

"Well, I'll be down in about an hour." Ap had gone home to spend the night with the kids once they knew Bella was coming out of her coma. "You can turn around and take my truck back up and sleep and bathe and spend some time."

"Yeah. Okay." Except the thought made his belly hurt. What if she got worse while he was gone?

"Hey, the other kids need us too. I'll stay with her, you know that."

"I know." He did know, but he worried.

"Well, you stay right there, and I'll be down." Ap sounded better, more rested.

"Sure. I'll be here."

"Love you." Ap hung up, and Trey sat back, rolling his head on his neck.

He was beginning to learn this new normal. Bella was losing patience, was feeling good enough to be frustrated and angry.

She didn't remember getting kicked at all. In fact, she remembered zero from the day before the accident.

And she was refusing to believe she needed to rest and recover. Which she so did with a hole in her head.

Miss Traynor came out with a weak smile. "She's not a happy camper, Trey, but she can read, do math. That part is just like it has been."

"Yeah. They say it may manifest more in her temper and balance for a bit." He smiled back, rising to shake her hand.

"She's always had a bit of a temper, sir."

"A bit? She gets that from the McIntosh side."

"Does she?" She chuckled. "Well, good luck. I look forward to seeing her back at school."

"I'm praying she'll be back after the break. Will someone at the school help me work it out?"

"Absolutely." She dug in her purse for a card, then handed it right over. "Call Mrs. Gonzales."

"I can do that. Thank you for coming down. I know she loves you." *Or at least tolerates you.*

"She tries." She left him, and Trey steeled himself to go back in there.

It was like facing a little pissed-off, bored lion.

He washed his hands, then went in. "Hey, baby girl."

"I want to go home."

"Me too. I think it'll be soon. You're like the miracle girl. You're working so hard."

"No, now." Her face got all red.

"Hey. I know, but you were really hurt. So hurt you scared me really bad. The doctors get the final say." He kept his voice calm.

"You're the daddy!"

"I am, and it's my job to keep you safe as I can."

Her lower lip pooched out. "But—"

He stared. He didn't say another word; he just stared.

"I hate you."

He snorted. "Liar. You hate being stuck in bed."

"I do." Tears welled up in her eyes. "Why do I have to be hurted?" She sounded like Courtney more than her twelve-year-old self. The more upset she got, the more words she lost.

"Breathe, chica." He sat on the end of the bed, holding her gaze. "Sometimes cowboys take a fall, right? What counts is that we get back up, brush off the sand, and get in the saddle."

"Right. Like when Uncle Ap falled and broke his... his...."

"Collarbone," he offered.

"When Uncle Ap broke his collarbone and still rode."

"That's right. You get up and you ride. That's the cowboy way."

"What else is the cowboy way?"

He grinned. How many times had they talked about this? "A cowboy lives each day honest and brave. A cowboy always does his best. A cowboy keeps his promises, always. A cowboy stands up for what is right and good. A cowboy is tough and fair. And more than anything, a cowboy loves his family, his animals, his land, and his God."

"You're a cowboy too, Uncle Daddy. I don't hate you. Am I going to get to walk again today?"

"I sure hope so." They wanted her moving, but the physical therapists wanted to be there with her still. "You've been trying so hard. Uncle Ap is coming to visit you." He leaned close. "I need to go home and have a shower. I smell like a gorilla!"

She squealed, just as likely to be overly amused as overly angry. "I like gorillas. But I love Uncle Ap too. Can he bring a game?"

"I'll tell him." He whipped out his phone to text: *Bring the Sorry game.*

On it.

"He's on it. Have you thought about what you want to eat for lunch today?"

"Can I have a sandwich?"

"Of course you can." Whew. Breakfast had been… plate tossing.

"With tuna fish?"

"Oh, the tuna fish here is very good. I like mine with pickles."

"I like pickles and lettuce."

"Fries or carrots?"

"Fries with ketchup?" He loved that he got a smile.

"Yes, ma'am. Shall I call?"

"Please?" She didn't bounce, exactly, but it was a close thing.

"You want milk? Orange juice? Apple juice?" He lowered his voice. "Want to share a Sprite?"

"Oh…." She almost looked like a cartoon kid, her eyes wide. "Yes."

"Rock on. Don't tell Uncle Ap, 'kay?"

"I swear."

He called for lunch, adding some apple slices and peanut butter for him. At least this place had decent food, and he could afford it.

By the time lunch was done, Ap showed up with the Sorry! game, a huge stuffed rhinoceros, and the Uno cards.

"You're loaded for bear."

"I'm the fun uncle."

He would have swatted Ap if the man hadn't been laughing.

"Uncle Ap, I want to go home."

"I know, baby girl." Ap sat on the bed with her. "I need a kiss."

She leaned forward carefully and kissed him. "I did it this time."

"You did!" Ap rubbed her arm gently. Big hugs were discouraged until her head healed. "Have you had a good day?"

"I had a bad morning, but I ate tuna fish for lunch and I want my walk soon."

"Oh cool. Then we can nap and maybe play a game after. You know Uncle Daddy is going to spend the night at home, right? You're stuck with me." Ap looked a little worried, which he knew would make Bella jump to his defense.

"We can talk about my barrel horse. We're not naming him Roland."

"Okay. I knew you heard us." Ap winked at Trey. "You can't name him Trigger either."

"What if she's a girl? Is that mine? Can I hold her?"

"You can." Ap handed over the toy before coming to kiss him. "Mmm, tuna."

"Yes. Hey, stranger. How's things?"

"The kids are better now that they know she's awake and in there." Ap smiled. "There's enough food at the house for ten families."

"Tamales?" He could murder a few dozen tamales.

"Red pork and green chicken. I asked Dolores for black bean and goat cheese like I had in Austin, and she hit me."

"Yeah, you have to watch that hipster shit."

"Uncle Daddy! You curseded." Bella was bouncing her rhino gently.

"I owe you a dollar." He had to grin. She was getting better, day by day.

Ap winked at him, beaming, and he could see the relief in Ap's eyes. "All that food and I still forgot to eat. Y'all mind if I have my Subway?" Ap had another bag tucked back.

He inhaled. Ah, spicy Italian. He knew it well.

"Go for it." He started gathering his things so he could do some laundry when he got home.

"Cool." Ap pulled out his sandwich. "So, did you share a Sprite?"

Bella went wide-eyed. "Would we do that?"

"Uh-huh. You would, and you would both try to hide it. That just means cookie after nap and not now."

Yeah, they had to watch her sugar.

Trey winked over at his girl, and she grinned wide, happy to play along. That was what he wanted to see.

"Okay, Bella. You have a good afternoon, okay? I'll be back tomorrow."

She nodded, her smile fading only a little. "Will the other kids ever come see me?"

"Yes. We're coming Saturday. The whole crew."

"Okay." She brightened right up again.

"Courtney is all jealous. She found out you get room service." Ap worked on his sandwich. "I got this, baby. Go on."

"You be good, okay? Walk with Janet. I'm ready for you to come home."

"I am too. Love you, Uncle Daddy." She made her rhino wave.

"Love you, baby girl. Love you, Ap. I'll call in a bit." It took everything he had to leave, but he did. He needed a nap, a shower, a real shave, and to hold his other babies and hear about their days.

Then he would spell Ap, assuming he made it through the night.

THEY sang. Bella walked. They both napped. One round of Sorry! before dinner came, and now Bella was sound asleep while he watched Food Network. It was a lot like being in a hotel.

Ap finally felt like he could breathe. This he knew; this he'd done. He'd sat in a thousand hospitals with a zillion cowboys, watching them come back.

God help him, he never wanted it to be his kids again.

Ever. He wanted them all to be safe forever.

He knew better, but still, he could wish.

His phone rang, Cole's number showing. Panic hit him hard, and he answered, praying he hadn't jinxed them. "What's up, son?"

"Hey. Uncle Daddy went to sleep on the sofa at like, five. I fed everybody, and they're in bed, but… do I wake him up?"

"Yeah. Wake him up, make him eat something, and send him to bed." He breathed, which was nice, because he was a little light-headed with relief.

"Okay. How's Bella?"

"She's kind of amazing. She's sleeping right now, which is good. She had a busy day. How's all of you?"

"Okay. Busy. There's all the end-of-year stuff. We need to decorate for Christmas, you know? The kids are asking if we're going to."

"We totally are. If we have to, Uncle Daddy can do the inside stuff with you guys, and I can come do the outside." He sighed. God, he hoped Bella could be home. He knew she wanted that more than anything.

So did he. So did Trey.

Shit, he wanted him and Trey to sleep in the same damn bed.

"That's cool. Is she going to be home by Christmas?"

"I hope so, kiddo. I mean, her skull is a mess, but her brain is pretty intact." Thank God. He hadn't been a real Catholic in a long time, but he crossed himself.

"Is she bald?"

"Just a spot. It'll grow out before school starts."

"I'll have to tease her, though." Cole sounded relieved more than anything.

"Yeah. Hey, have I said thank you for everything you've done, kiddo? I'm so proud of you."

"I'm just…." Cole sighed. "I'm ready to get out of here, you know? Two more years."

"I know. Don't rush it, man. It will come." God, Cole was so teenager, ready to run.

"You sound like Uncle Daddy. I'm not going to get stuck here, though. I'm going to get out."

"Okay. Just promise you'll come visit. We love you."

"Sure. This is home, huh? You know that. You get to travel." Cole sounded so young, so much like Trey back in the beginning.

Back in the beginning. Shit. Trey was only twelve years older than Cole, not thirty.

"I do. I miss it every day. Give it time, and if you decide to go, you do." Cole would go to college, if nothing else.

"Eh, I can't leave Uncle Daddy right now, man. By the time I head to college, Braden will be driving and can help with the girls. I'm going to warm up some enchilada casserole and feed him. You're all good?"

"I'm all good."

"Okay. Love you."

"Love you too, kiddo." He hung up, then took a deep, deep breath.

Christ, his head hurt.

The door opened, and the night nurse poked her head in. "She's okay?"

"She's fine."

"Okay. Holler if you need us." The nurse popped back out.

"Are you crying, Uncle Ap?" Bella's voice was sleepy. "Do you want my rhinoserious?"

"I'm not." He scooted over, took her hand. "How are you? Hurting?"

"Uh-uh. I want to go home to my bed and Courtney."

"Yeah? Not Amelia?"

"No, she would just cry a lot."

He laughed. "What about Braden?"

She pouted. "I'm mad at him."

"Why?"

"I... I don't know. I can't remember."

"Oh." He moved from the couch to sit on the bed. "Well, you'll get over it, I bet."

"Uh-huh." She held on to him. "When I grow up, I'm going to be a cowboy like you."

"You're a cowboy now, baby girl. I couldn't be more proud. Now, you'll have to think twice about doctoring a horse that needs a vet or a farrier, but you're a cowboy."

"Yeah. Yeah. No more of that. Uncle Daddy says I'll have to wear a helmet when I ride for a while."

"Yep. And when you do anything else that might endanger your little noggin." He hugged her. Screw the advice from the docs. He wasn't gonna squeeze her head.

"Do I have to wear it to school? The kids will tease me."

"I don't know, kiddo. The doctors will tell us. But if you do, you just tell those kids you almost died. Then you'll be amazing."

"Uncle Daddy said I was in an ambulance, with sirens and everything. I wish I could remember that part."

"You were hurt." He had to smile at her wanting to know all the details.

"Yeah." She blinked slowly. "But I'm going to be home soon."

"You so will. Especially if you keep doing as good at therapy as today." He eased her back down on her pillows. "You're so brave."

"I'm a cowboy like you and Uncle Daddy. We're brave."

"We are." Except when they were terrified.

Except when their babies were hurt. Or when they lost their entire families in one fell swoop.

Ap closed his eyes, sending up a little prayer. No more of that, please.

In fact, just goodness, from now on. Only goodness. It was coming up on Christmas, after all.

Chapter Twenty-One

"UNCLE Daddy! When are they coming?"

Jesus fucking Christ. Why did they tell you they were going to let you go and take thirty hours to do it?

"Soon, I'm sure, baby girl. Patience."

"I'm tired of being good."

"I can tell." He gave her the dad look.

She began to tear up. "You're always mad at me! You're always grumpy!"

"Hey! No yelling, huh?" Ap came in from the hallway. "They have her discharge papers. They're coming in a few."

"With a wheelchair?" Bella asked.

"Yes. They said it was a special one." Ap looked at him, smiling a little. "You okay?"

"Yes." They'd had a huge meltdown yesterday during the PICC line removal, and that had caused a bit of a panic when Bella started throwing up. Today, he just wanted to go home.

"Cool. We're almost there, huh? Don't lose faith now."

Trey wasn't sure if Ap was talking to him or Bella. Hell, he wasn't sure it mattered.

"Everyone's going to miss you here, Bella. All the nurses and doctors." See him, see him be positive.

"Uh-huh." She was still damp around the eyes and pouty at the lips. "I didn't do it on purpose, Uncle Daddy."

"No one ever once said you did, girl."

"But you're so mad!"

"No, he's tired." Ap went to hug her. "Down in his bones. We're going to take him home and put him to bed."

"Who will take care of us?"

"Me!" Ap looked comically shocked.

"Oh, but you're still an amateur." She giggled.

"An ama.... Did you hear this?"

Trey began to laugh, tickled to death.

They all hooted, and the guy finally came with a wheelchair, and it was bright and covered in pink glitter.

"Oh, ride in style!"

"Oh wow. Wow." Bella's eyes went wide.

"I'll go get the truck, Trey."

"Okay, you need to put on your helmet, baby girl." He wasn't going to take any chuff about this.

Her face screwed up, but she sighed before letting him slip it over her head. "I feel like Cole at a game."

"Oh, I like it. We have to protect your head for the next few weeks." Possibly longer. Whatever. "The important part is that you'll be home, right?"

"I will." She got all determined-sounding. "I won't do anything to make it scary, I swear."

He went for honesty. "Honey, just driving you home scares me." Trey grinned at her.

"Yeah, I bet Uncle Ap will drive."

"I bet he will." He grabbed her bag and his laptop case. "Tallyho!"

"On Dancer, on Prancer!" Bella laughed and pointed to the door.

"On Gonzales and Enrique!" He got it. He wanted to go home.

The nurse tech snorted. "I'm José."

"On José!" He grinned over, and they all three cracked up. They headed down the elevator, to the big lobby. The truck was there, humming in the cold, waiting for them.

Ap hopped out to come around and open the back passenger door. "There she is."

"Yep. Time to head home." He could cry with relief. Ap had the entire back seat loaded with comforters and pillows, to pad her in all directions.

"I'll drive, baby." Ap gave him a sweet smile.

"Works for me. The kids excited?" It would be around five thirty by the time they made it home, so they'd need to stop and pick up McDonald's or something.

He would bet Bella would love Mickey D's after all those tuna and chicken sandwiches.

"They are. Even Cole is staying home after work." Ap made sure Trey was in before hopping back in the truck.

He looked back at Bella. "You okay?"

"Mmm-hmm." She was already half asleep.

He reached out to touch Ap's arm as soon as they pulled out of the chaos. "Home, James."

"You know it. I'm gonna cut across on University. There was an accident on 25."

"God, just what we need." He turned on the radio and leaned back, his eyes feeling like they were filled with grit.

Ap hummed along with the radio, and Trey was reminded that 90 percent of Ap's job was driving.

He wanted to say so many things, but he didn't want to talk. He wanted to just… be.

Ap patted his thigh. "Put your head back and rest, baby. I'll get you home."

"I believe in you. I feel like… I'm fixin' to shatter a little."

"I know." Ap did know; of that he was damn sure.

"The kids are out of school after today." They were so behind. Thank God there were two of them, him and Ap. They could play catch-up together.

"Well, I made Amelia's one party last night." Ap snickered. "Man, I was a fish out of water."

"And you were at the choir concert. I made the Girl Scouts party and the end of season team bash."

"We did okay."

"Yeah, we even made the hall party at the children's ward." He did put his head back, a sigh escaping him. "Go us."

"Rest, baby. We got a ways to go."

"I know. I want to keep you company. I want to…." God, he wanted to be home.

"I'm fine. I can see you right there, and you have no idea how much that improves the drive."

Okay, his cheeks went hot, but fuck, that was fine to hear. "Tell me we get to sleep together in the same bed tonight, honey?"

"We do or something awful is going to happen. At my hand."

"Yeah. I need it." Not even sex, although that would be welcome. He just needed contact. He needed to be held.

"Me too. God, I've seen you most every day, but I missed you."

"Yes." Everything had been wrong, but it was going to be right now. They would make it so out of sheer will and have Christmas for the kids in the nick of time.

He closed his eyes for just a second, just a heartbeat, and then he was gone. Simply floated away.

AP hoped that nap in the truck had done Trey some good. Dinner had been achieved, the kids were in bed, and Christmas lights twinkled on the tree they'd all waited to decorate until Bella got home.

He was damn ready for adult time.

Trey wandered up and down the long hall, peeking in at the little girls, leaving the boys to their games and phones.

Ap walked up behind him so he could grab that fine, tight ass. Trey jumped for him, but he didn't pull away or turn around. He just kept moving them toward the bedroom.

"Shh. Just walk, baby. We're locking the door. Bella has her night hat on and is sound asleep." She had taken her pain pill, and she was out for the count. Now he needed to take care of his man.

Trey looked less than convinced when they entered the bedroom, but when Ap locked the door, then turned back for a kiss, Trey gave right in, melting against him. Those long arms wrapped around him, Trey holding him close.

They trembled together for a minute, and then the strong arms around him tightened, drawing him to the bed.

Ap followed eagerly, wanting anything he could get. Skin or kisses or just rubbing off like teenagers.

"Can we be naked?" Trey asked, the question so needy. "Please."

"Before we get too busy. Good idea." Ap started tossing off clothes, and Trey followed suit, baring the huge, gorgeous body to his gaze.

He wanted to climb Trey like a mountain, but when he tried they toppled to the bed, laughing.

"I swear to God, we'd better not wake the kids." Trey laughed for him, the sound muffled in their kiss.

"Shhh." He kissed Trey again and again, feeling wild, like finally being in their bed had broken a dam. He shimmied up Trey's body, framing his lover's face with his hands.

"Hey." Trey smiled for him, a real, happy smile that made him feel ten feet tall.

Ap rubbed their noses together. "Hey, baby."

"I love you."

Oh. Oh, bald and sure and honest. He sort of wanted to holler with his joy.

"I love you too." Because he did, with the passion of when they were just kids and the surety of the man he was now.

"Good." Lord, that goofy, wonderful smile made him grin back. "I love this—touching you."

Trey squeezed his ass, proving exactly what Trey wanted to touch.

"It's been too damn long, baby." He nipped at Trey's neck, wanting a taste. Trey lifted his chin, offering himself over, even as Trey began to rub them together.

He licked and kissed his way down to one collarbone, feeling decadent. Fuzzy man. Christ, Trey was like a dream, heavy and broad beneath him. He plucked at a bit of chest hair, then soothed by rubbing those tiny nipples.

Then he did it again, laughing as Trey bucked and jerked. "This is more fun than color TV."

"Good. I would hate to be replaced by cable."

He kissed Trey's mouth again, jumping when Trey slid a finger between his asscheeks.

Trey stilled. "No?"

"Yes. Anything." He could catch as well as pitch; Trey knew that well enough. It just took him by surprise.

"Just want to touch you, feel you." Trey drew circles at the small of his back, sensitizing his nerves.

He arched, poking his butt out a little. "I want that too. I'm kind of oral, so I want to kiss and lick."

Trey's lips quirked. "I remember that about you. Fondly."

"Do you? I'm willing to prove it again." He bent to lick at the nipples he'd touched, each in turn. They drew up for him, wrinkling up tight as the cold air hit them. So fine. He stroked down the flat belly, fingers dancing over Trey's abs. The muscles rolled and jerked under his touch, and then Trey grabbed his head, encouraging him to suck, to lick those needy nipples.

Someone liked that a lot. So Ap gave what Trey needed. He licked at each one, went back to draw the first between his lips and pull hard.

"Jesus. Jesus, Ap. Please." Trey wrapped one heavy leg over him, pressing them tight together.

"I got you." He said it against that sweet skin, then bit. Not as hard as he would like, but he was easing them into it.

Trey nodded, the huge chest rising and falling like a grand bellows. The man loved sensation, loved to feel everything Ap gave him, and that hadn't changed a bit over the years.

"I should have done this years ago," Trey moaned. "I should have taken you to bed and let you turn me inside out."

"I was so careful." Ap hadn't wanted to upset the kids, especially Cole, and he'd been afraid Trey would turn him down.

"I was stuck. Mad. Whatever. I want more, Ap."

"More." He licked down Trey's belly, aiming for the thick cock that pressed against him. Oh, he wanted that, wanted to taste the heavy cock between his lips. He opened up, running his tongue along the underside.

Trey spread for him, one leg drawing up and out, spreading wide. That gave him room to slide one hand under the heavy balls when he closed his lips around Trey's shaft and sucked deep.

"Ap." His name had never sounded so fine, not in anyone else's voice. He wanted to hear that every night, forever. Right now, he just wanted to hear it over and over. He licked as he bobbed up and down, then sucked hard at the head. Ap knew that spot just underneath would drive Trey mad.

A flood of need poured from Trey's lips, then followed from the aching cock, hot seed spilling into him.

Damn. Oh damn, that was the best thing ever. That Trey was that hot off the mark for him. He licked his lover clean, not at all worried. Trey wouldn't lie to him about his lack of lovers.

Trey moaned softly before dragging him up, rocking them together as Trey plundered his mouth, kissing him like there was nothing Trey needed more.

His cock ached, his asscheeks clenched, and he knew it wouldn't be long. Trey grabbed his cock in one hand and reached down with the other and pressed one finger into his hole, the scrape enough to make his eyes roll.

His toes curled, his breath caught, and he almost lost it, but Ap held on, wanting just a few more minutes of this amazing pleasure.

"Got you." Trey kept touching him, kissing him, pushing at him. "Lord, I got you, and I intend to keep you."

"Please. Promise." He panted, his hips sawing back and forth, pushing. Needing.

"Swear to God." Trey latched on to the curve of his neck and began to suck, pulling up a mark.

"Oh Jesus. Oh fuck. Trey." He lost it, thrusting into Trey's hand until he stifled a shout, his ears ringing as he came.

Trey kept him close, holding him like he was precious.

Ap hoped he was. God knew he was so far gone for Trey he was in deep trouble.

"We're home." Trey sighed the words against his throat. "Thank God."

He stroked the long line of Trey's spine. "It's been a long couple of weeks, to be sure."

"Yes." Trey kissed him again, slow and sweet. "God yes."

"What do you want for Christmas, baby?" Ap asked.

"You. I want you." Trey sighed, the sound purely exhausted, but happy, Ap thought.

"You got that for sure." He would be happy to give Trey that present over and over.

Trey patted his ass, then melted underneath him, sound asleep, just like that.

He laughed softly before rearranging them so he held Trey with one arm while he lay on his back. There had to be some cheesy Christmas movie on TV.

This was so much nicer than sleeping in what was now Cole's bedroom and jacking off to infomercials.

So much better.

He kissed the top of Trey's head and closed his eyes. He knew what he would dream about tonight.

Chapter Twenty-Two

IT started snowing on the twenty-third, heavy wet shit that made the slog from the house to the barn miserable.

Trey couldn't snarl too much, though. The girls were having a ball, and Braden was proving that he was going to be one hell of a pitcher.

"God *damn* it, Braden! If you hit Bella with another snowball, I'm going to beat your ass!"

Hmm. Ap sounded a little stressed.

He moved deeper into the barn, letting himself pretend he hadn't heard. Ap could handle it. He needed to learn how to ride herd on kids as well as animals.

God, he loved having someone else here, another adult to help with all this mess—from the house to the kids to the animals and all the work. It made life feel... lighter.

Not to mention the nookie. God knew, that was a fine thing.

He'd never had that—hot and cold running sex. Hand jobs in the barn. Blowjobs in the shower. Wild kisses that made him dizzy whenever Ap caught him.

Crazy. Crazy, but wonderful.

"Jesus Christ, I can't wait to get on the road again." Ap slammed the barn door, then blinked up, obviously surprised to see him. "Hey, baby."

"Hey. I was checking the hay." He knew his cheeks were burning; he could feel it. God, he was a bit of an idiot, sitting in here and mooning like a calf when Ap was aching to escape. Fuck. "I'm going to have to run out in a bit and take Cole to work and get some of the last-minute errands done. You need anything?"

"A cup of sanity? I swear to God, Braden is trying to kill Bella. Because he can. How do you do this full-time?"

He tried to chuckle, but it didn't really work. How? Because he didn't have a choice. Because he'd been the one with no skills and nothing to offer, so he'd muddled along until he'd figured it out, sort of. "I guess they have guilt to work out. I'll take him and the little ones with me, if you'll stay here with Bella. She's not up to errands yet."

"Sure." Ap gave him the stink eye. "You okay?"

"Yeah. Feet are cold is all." *Fine. I'm fucking fine. I was standing in here half-hard because I was pretending that you wanted to be stuck here with me as much as I wanted you stuck here with me. Now I feel like a fool.* At least no one else knew.

"Yeah, it's gray and soggy." Ap shook his head, looking sorrowful as a lost calf.

"The sun'll come back. Give it time." He finished his check, lingering in the shadows in the farthest reach of the barn. "I'll pick up all the stuff for Christmas Eve and the day of."

He had a list.

"Oh. Sure." Now Ap looked a little put out, lips pressed together.

Did he ask what was wrong? He knew what it was— Ap was already frustrated. Ap was bored. Ap was here.

Did he not ask and come off as a fucker? Jesus, he was tired, and his head hurt.

One day he'd be old, the kids would be gone, and he wouldn't have to do Christmas anymore.

Oh, that sounded... lonely as fuck.

"You okay?" That was fair, right?

"I'm fine. I was just thinking we could go shop together, but I figure you want to get stuff done. No big." Except the tight set of Ap's shoulders said different.

"How? I can't leave Bella alone, Cole has a shift tonight and tomorrow morning, and he can't drive in this snow in that POS he drives." This was why he needed another adult here. "I can call Dolores and see if she'll come over for a few hours and watch everyone...."

If she wasn't busy with her eighty-seven-thousand grandbabies and making her own posole.

"No, I got it. I'm not good for much else, I know, but I can watch TV with Bella." Ap snapped it out, just snake mean.

"Oh, for fuck's sake, stop being an asshole. You want to go so bad, go, but you'll fucking stick around for Christmas for these kids. I gave up my entire fucking life to raise them; you can give up the road for two more motherfucking days." He stormed for the door, so hurt and mad he couldn't hardly bear it, knowing that he had to. He had to get a boy to work and buy groceries and last-minute presents and tape and wrangle kids and feed them before getting them all home, feeding critters, and heading back out to pick Cole up.

Ap grabbed his arm and spun him around, both of them nearly going ass over teakettle. "No, sir. Don't you say that to me and walk away. I've been here every Christmas. Every year, even when it would have been easier to go from finals right down to Fort Worth. You don't want me around, fine, you say so, but they're my kids too."

"Easier? You drive right through here to get to Texas, and we both know it. Easier not to stop, maybe, but don't bullshit me. I don't even know why you're so goddamn ready to go." *To leave me to all this alone, again.*

"I'm not! I'm just frustrated with the kids! Jesus, asshole, why are you snarling at me?"

"Because I—" *Because I love you so much that I'd let you go, and you don't love me enough to stay.* The thought was too big to say, too hard, and it wouldn't matter if he said it out loud or not. He closed his eyes and swallowed down the bile in his throat. "Shit, I guess I'm just in a mood. Told you, my feet are all froze. I'm getting old for this winter shit."

Hell, he was the oldest twenty-eight-year-old on earth.

"Uh-huh." Ap sighed. "Go on and get Cole to work, and all. Bella and I are getting to be pros at playing board games."

"Yeah. I—"

"I got to get to work! Just let me drive; I can do it!" Cole was in his uniform, face like a thundercloud.

"This weather is—" There was no way. No way.

"I'm not a baby! I have to go!"

"Let me get the kids." He headed back toward the house to gather his wallet and keys and kids, when all hell broke loose.

"I want to stay here and play outside!"

"Me too!"

"I'm staying here and playing my game."

"I'm going."

"Goddamn it!" he roared. "Will y'all shut up!"

They all stopped, wide-eyed, and stared at him. Cole looked like he might snarl, but Trey leveled a finger at him. "Not one word. Go get in the truck."

"The girls can stay with me. Braden, go with Uncle Daddy and help him do the shopping." Ap was quiet, but there was steel there.

He stomped inside, took a handful of Excedrin Migraine, and grabbed his phone, wallet, and keys. "Text me if you think of anything you need. I'll be back."

If they were lucky, he wouldn't kill either one of his sons or any random asshole at Walmart on the way.

"WHY are you and Uncle Daddy fighting?" Bella asked him once Trey and the boys were gone.

Ap shook his head. "I have no idea, baby girl. Stress, I guess? Who wants hot cocoa?" Bella needed to get inside, but if he flat out said that, she would balk.

"I want to build a snowman!" Courtney said, but her little teeth were chattering.

"I want cocoa. Can we make cookies to surprise Uncle Daddy?" Amelia watched him like she wasn't sure if he was friend or foe. God, she got that from Trey, that watching thing.

"I think that sounds perfect. You want to make cookies, Court?" He looked at the sky. "Trust me, there will be way more snow tomorrow."

"Come on, Court. My head hurts. I want to go watch *Elf* and warm up. Can you start the fire?"

"I can if you take a Benadryl. No sneezing. Your brain might fall out."

"Ew!" Bella laughed for him, though, and he hugged her, leading them all inside.

They dealt with coats and boots and hats and mittens, and then he settled Ames with a tablet to look up recipes and started milk on the stove while Bella and Courtney curled up on the couch.

"Don't forget the fire!" Bella called.

"I won't." He had to watch the milk first, though. God, how did Trey do this? As much as he seemed to feel he wasn't good at much, Trey had his undying admiration for not eating their young early on.

"Do you think we should make chocolate chip or peanut butter?" Ames asked.

Were those good for Christmas? Didn't Christmas cookies have to be sugar cookies with things? Or biscochitos? "Uh, what does Uncle Daddy like best?"

"Uh... Bella? What cookies does Uncle Daddy like?" Ames hollered.

"Biscochitos! In bear shapes!"

"Oh, Cole has to make those. They have booze." Amelia looked stricken.

"Hmm. Your daddy liked peanut butter with chocolate chips. How about we do that?"

"Okay. Okay…. Oh! Oh, do we have Kisses? We could do the ones with Kisses!"

"Let me look." Sure enough, they had a pack of Kisses in the cabinet where Trey kept the chocolate stash. "Boom."

"Yay! We'll make those and then see. Uncle Daddy will be so surprised!"

"Works for me!" He knew Trey would make a big deal of sugar cookies tomorrow, but he honestly thought biscochitos came from the neighbors....

Hell, they might be coming from the Walmart. How did he know?

A knock came to the front door, a vaguely familiar man standing there when he opened it. "Can I help you?"

"Hey. I'm Ray. Ray Griegos. I know you guys have been having some trouble—with the hospital and all. So we took up a collection at the church. I got a bunch of stuff in the truck."

Ap blinked. Then he grinned. "That's super nice. Hi, Ray. I'm Ap. I think we met at a game."

"We did. I'm a friend of Trey's, sorry." Ray held one hand out. "Pleased to meet you again. I'm sure glad you could come home. I know it's hard for you two, having to raise the kids. It was a blessing that they have you. They would have been split all up in foster care."

God, he'd never even thought of that. "Trey's been amazing. Let's see what you got." They shook hands, but he peered at Ames before he went outside. "Count out and unwrap Kisses until I get back."

"Yes, sir. Hey, Mr. Ray!"

"Hey, Amelia-Bedelia!" Ray raised a hand. "I'll come in and say hi in a second, okay? I got goodies from Marcella for you."

"Thank you!" She started counting Kisses, so Ap followed Ray out to the truck.

It was filled with wrapped presents for the kids, along with fleece blankets and boxes of cookies and two-liters of soda. In the back of the truck was a giant turkey and a huge pan marked tamales.

"Oh man. This is all for us? Are you sure?" He felt a little guilty.

"I know that you had to leave the finals early, so we wanted to help. You know, Trey's always telling us how you're his hero, and we all hear about how you ride."

A warm bud of happiness uncurled in his belly. "Yeah? I do okay."

"More than okay. You're famous. I know." Ray started unloading the truck, the snow powdering his jacket. "We just wanted to help. God knows Trey never turns anyone down, and he's the first one to volunteer to help."

"He is." Famous? "I'm not exactly all that, Ray."

"Mira, look. You are around here. Should I put things on Trey's porch?"

"Yeah, please. I can get them in the rest of the way." He grabbed a load himself.

"Uncle Ap?" Bella stuck her head out the door. "Hi, Ray!"

"Get your head back inside, baby girl."

"Hey, Bella. I'll come in in a second. Get your butt in the house."

"Okay! I saved the milk."

"Good girl." Ap waved her inside and grabbed more stuff out of the truck. He would text Trey and tell him not to get another big bird unless they were on sale. Or tamales. Or posole. Christ.

They probably didn't need to make biscochitos for three years. "I don't even know what to say, man."

"Merry Christmas works for me."

"Well, Merry Christmas for sure. I'm sure Trey will call you too. Come on in and have a hot chocolate?"

"I will. I need to see my girls. I have a little box of candies for all of them." Ray helped him get the food inside and in the freezer and fridge. "Eee-a-la, it's all snow out there, eh?"

"It's getting bad."

Bella had saved the milk and melted the Abuelita in it. Good going. "Marshmallows?"

"Please." Ray grinned at him. "How you feeling? Better?"

"Better. I played in the snow." And she looked exhausted now.

"You gonna have a cookie and go sit on the couch?" Ap handed out cups of cocoa but gave Bella a pointed look.

"Uh-huh." She hugged Ray. "Thank you for coming. Uncle Daddy will call you. We love you."

"Love you too, hon." Ray glanced at him. "Trey out running errands?"

"Yessir. Taking Cole to work. He hasn't had enough practice with this kind of weather."

"How many more Kisses, Uncle?"

He looked at Amelia. "I think that's enough, kiddo."

The pile of foil and chocolate was... impressive. "Don't let the dogs get into any of that."

"Okay." She glared at the corgis.

"It's good to see Trey out and about without all the kids. That ought to make things so much easier."

"We're easy!" Ames said. "We're good."

"You are, but sometimes a man needs just grown-ups, right, mija?"

"You're a grown-up. Can Victoria come spend the night?"

"Maybe after Christmas, Amelia, hmm?"

"Okay!" She hummed, piling up wrappers and taking them to the trash can.

Ray drained his cocoa. "Okay, I got to hit the road. Need any more help getting anything inside?"

"No. No, thank you so much." He shook hands again.

"Anytime. You tell Trey to holler. We'll get together in a few days."

"You got it." He walked Ray to the door, still a little stunned.

"Can we open presents?" Amelia asked when he came back.

"No. Those are for Christmas morning. Let's make these cookies." A peek told him that Bella was sound asleep and Court was coloring.

"Okay!" God, that was a beautiful smile. Seriously. "I'll get the peanut butter! Can there be Christmas carols?"

"There totally can." All she really wanted to do was spend time with him. "Ferb! No."

She giggled softly. "Sneaky puppy."

"We don't want a sick puppy." He moved the chocolate back away from the edge of the table.

"No. No, Bella was hard enough. No more."

"Exactly." He texted Trey real quick about the food.

It felt amazing, how their neighbors just came together for them. Ap would get to know them all, which he was actually looking forward to.

Hopefully Trey was looking forward to that same thing.

Chapter Twenty-Three

"MORE coffee?"

"Please." Trey smiled at the evening manager—Jaycelle, he thought—and watched Braden play on his phone. They'd gotten all their errands done, but it had taken forever, and before he knew it, it was seven o'clock, and Cole got off at eight, and there was no way for him to get home and back here.

So they sat.

Fuck-a-doodle-goddamn-doo.

"That's some weather out there, huh?" She poured him another cup before handing Braden another water. He'd only been allowed one Coke.

"Yes, ma'am. It's getting heavy. As soon as Cole's done, we're going to head out." *Or as soon as you let him loose, you harridan. He's a sixteen-year-old kid, for God's sake.*

"Oh, he's just got a few more minutes. It's so important to teach them responsibility."

What? Fuck that shit. He would find Cole another job, maybe at a feed store, where the hours didn't suck so hard. He kept it mild when he raised a brow. "I think Cole's a pretty responsible kid."

"All parents think that."

"Get your shit together, Braden. Cole? You ready to go? We got us a drive." He wasn't going to be ugly, but damn.

"Uh, Uncle Daddy?"

"Come on." He gave Cole a look, and Cole half grinned before taking off his apron.

"Night," Cole said.

"We'll talk about this tomorrow, Cole."

"Yeah, I don't think so," Trey muttered under his breath. Tomorrow Cole was calling and quitting.

Braden looked up, blinking hard when snow hit his face. "Wow, look at the snow."

"I know, right?" God, he wished he had his chains. "Let's go, boys. Chugga chugga."

Shit, it was way worse now than it had been a few hours ago. All he had to do was make it to the ranch. Hell, if he made it to the bottom of their road, he could call Ap to bring chains.

The man had been texting him all day.

It had been... well, a lot of it had been good, hadn't it?

They started out, creeping along, tires sliding on the ice. He turned the Christmas music on, straddling the centerline, because nobody was out here.

"I'm glad I didn't drive," Cole said quietly.

"I would have been out of my mind loco worrying about those old tires on this." He was careful to keep any comment about Cole's driving out of it.

"They do kinda suck on slick." Cole held the door handle hard.

Yeah, this was a once in ten years kinda storm.

"They do. We've got everything we need for the next few days, tons of food, all the presents, wood for the fire. You looking forward to it? Having Christmas?" He kept the chatter light, easy, but when he headed around one of the curves and spun out, leaving them facing the wrong way, he had to take a couple deep breaths. "Cole, call your Uncle Ap and tell him we'll be a while."

"Yessir." Cole pulled out his phone, the light bright in the night.

"Are we okay?" Braden asked.

"We are. I just needed to get my head back on straight."

"Hey, Uncle Ap. No, we're okay. It's just really slow going out here. Might take us a while. Okay. I'll keep checking in. No, I'm pretty sure I quit. Okay. Later."

"Thanks, son. I didn't want him worrying." *Okay, Trey. Get your ass moving.*

"He wanted to know if we were bringing food home." Cole chuckled.

"Ah. Was he joking?"

"Yeah, he said we have enough for an army."

"Yeah, Ray and them brought a feast."

"We get some of that, right?" Braden sounded a little worried.

Cole snorted. "Dude, you had a hamburger and fries, a shake, and mozzarella sticks."

"Thirteen-year-old boys are always hungry. I'm sure you remember that." He got them moving, doing the world's most careful thirty-eight-point turn ever. "And yes. There is food for you, boy. I swear."

"Okay." Braden sat back, and the boys went quiet, the feeling in the air tense.

"We can do this." He would do this. He had his kids in the fucking truck. He would get them home safe.

"I know." Cole nodded firmly. "You got this."

He did. He'd been driving for way longer than Cole. He got them moving back along the main road. He turned off on Paseo de Pueblo, heading away from the highway. The snow was thicker here, less icy, so he got more traction for a bit.

As he relaxed, the boys did.

Of course, once they got farther out, it was going to get bad again, not that the boys needed to know that.

Chapter Twenty-Four

AP paced. He did it in the kitchen, so only Phineas and Ferb saw him, but he paced. Bella was in bed, and Court and Amelia were blanket-covered on the couch, waiting to show Trey the cookies.

They'd left Denny's at eight. It was nine fifteen, and it was a fifteen-minute drive. Twenty tops. Where the hell were they?

He'd texted Cole three times, but the last two times, he'd gotten dick all. Dammit. Surely there was signal. Right?

"Uncle Ap? My head hurts."

He whirled around, startled by Bella's low voice. "Sorry, kiddo, you surprised me."

"Can you look at it? Is it bleeding?"

He checked, but it looked fine, and she wasn't running a fever. "I bet it's the weather. My head always hurts when it snows so heavy. You want some of your pain medicine?"

"Uh-huh. Please."

"Sure thing. Then we put your night bonnet back on, huh?" That was probably part of it too. In the hospital she'd had this huge dressing putting pressure on it most of the time. It had to feel weird still, even after several days.

She sighed. "Yeah. Where's Uncle Daddy and the boys?"

"Still driving home. Ice and snow is hard." He should have hidden chains in Trey's truck, but they usually didn't need them unless they were going to a ski area or something.

"Yeah. It's crazy." He got her medicated and her hat on, and then he got her curled up with the other two, Christmas cartoons on the television.

Lights flashed in the kitchen window, and his heart jumped into his throat. *Please, God.*

He eased up, his heart beating even harder when the dogs didn't bark. They just whined at the back door.

He grabbed his boots and his coat. He needed to get them and all the stuff in.

Cole was already moving, opening the bed cover and pulling out bags. Braden was grabbing stuff out of the back seat, and Trey was sitting behind the wheel, pale as milk.

Ap ran out, slipping and sliding. He opened the driver's side door. "Baby? Are you okay?"

"Yeah. Yeah, just catching my breath." Trey looked over at him, smile shaky. "That was less than fun."

"I'm sorry." He helped Trey out of the truck when Trey was ready. "We got all the makings of a feast, though. And we don't have to leave again for days, assuming the kid did quit."

"I'm pretty sure I got the kid fired." Trey rolled his eyes. "I bought the entire Walmart."

"So did your friend Ray's people." He winked. "Here, Braden, let me take that."

"I got it, Uncle. There's more."

Man, Trey had been stress shopping.

"I'll get the next load, then." Bags, bags, and more bags filled the back.

Toilet paper and wrapping paper and food and, Christ…. Look at all that shit.

"I knew we'd be snowed in a few days." Trey grabbed some of the bags. "I'm staying home tomorrow."

"So am I." It would take a day to unpack.

Cole came back for another load. "Go on, Uncles. I got this."

"You sure?"

Cole snorted. "It's just snow. Uncle Daddy needs a beer."

"He does," Braden agreed.

"Well, come on, then."

Trey laughed. "I got to pee first."

"You could write your name in the snow," Braden teased.

"I'm not freezing my dick off to show off my penmanship to you hooligans."

Ap blinked at them, and then he began to cackle, hooting out of sheer relief.

Trey ran inside, and Ap carried in a load next to Braden. "You missed Mr. Ray."

"Yeah, he's Uncle Daddy's best friend. He's a good guy."

"He seems like it. Isn't he a little old to be Uncle's best friend?" Ray had to be forty-five, not thirty.

"Uncle Daddy's old. Not like you. Real old."

He blinked down at Braden. He was almost two years older than Trey. *What the hell?* "Hey, Amelia made cookies."

"Yeah? Cool. I could have some cookies." Braden ran in, beating feet, and Cole came back out.

"I got the rest, Uncle, no worries."

"Cool. Come get a cookie when you're done."

"I saw. Peanut butter kisses. I like those. Rock on."

Trey was in with the girls, checking on Bella and nodding at them, getting his hugs. His big, brave, goofy lover.

Ap smiled, loving how his family was safe and together and about to celebrate Christmas.

Trey moved into the kitchen, beginning to put things away, dragging bags back into his office, working doggedly.

"Hey." Ap caught him between runs. "What can I do?"

"I...." Trey blinked at him. "I don't know. Maybe make me something warm and leaded. That was a harsh drive."

"You got it." Leaded his ass. It was damn near ten. More like cocoa with booze.

Trey needed a little liquid lubrication, a shower, and a rubdown, or those muscles would be like frozen rope in the morning. That was a service he would happily provide. He moved to the kitchen to heat up the cocoa they'd saved.

The boys were demolishing cookies and laughing, telling "no shit, there we were" stories.

Trey came in, pulled out a chair to sit on, smiling at them.

"Here, guys." He served cocoa to the boys, then turned away to slip booze into Trey's cup.

"Thanks, Uncle." Cole grinned at him. "It's good to be home. You looking forward to tomorrow?"

"Tomorrow, Christmas Day, the day after."

"Me too." Cole kinda chortled. "I don't have to work. Guess I'll start looking for a job after the first."

"I'll call the feed store, maybe, huh?" Trey drank deep of his cocoa.

"Or maybe you can help with the odd jobs. You were doing okay with those, right?" Ap was starting to get it, at least a little.

"Yeah, I just liked a steady check." Cole shrugged. "It's nice to choose your own hours, though. Right?"

"You know it." He watched Trey, making sure he didn't give away the fact that Ap had spiked his drink. The only clue Trey gave was the way his shoulders slowly eased down from his ears. Better.

That drive had to have been horrendous.

"I'm gonna go play video games. Is that okay, Uncles?"

They both nodded at Braden, and he headed off.

Cole chuckled. "Good cookies. I'm gonna go call Julianne."

"Good deal. Thanks for your help." Trey sat there at the table, staring into nothing. "Thanks for the drink."

"You're welcome. Let me put the littles to bed. Why don't you go take a hot shower?" Trey needed it. He looked beat down.

"Yeah. Yeah, I think I will. It's been a long damn day." Trey reached out, touched his wrist. "Sorry about earlier. I'm just grumpy. I'll be back in a second."

Ap moved to the living room. "Okay, you two. You're asleep on the couch." He bent to lift Courtney. "Off to bed." He carried Court and let Amelia lean on him.

Bella held on to his belt, and together he got them all tucked in. Three little girls sleeping hard. After he let the dogs out and in, he went to lock up the house and turn off the TV, bank the fire and turn off the lights, and then he headed back to Trey.

Steam billowed out of the bathroom, and the water was still running, so he stripped off to step in with his lover. He wanted to soap Trey up and rub him down. Shit, he needed to reconnect, to figure out what was hurt and make it better.

He didn't know why Trey was so touchy, but he was gonna find out.

Trey blinked at him, gave him a smile. "Hey."

"Hey, baby. I can wash your back."

"That sounds nice." Trey turned, offering him that taut ass, those broad shoulders.

He 'bout near drooled. He soaped up his hands and rubbed Trey's back. Look at all that muscle. That man worked hard. And Trey was stiff and tense, fighting his touch for a bit.

"Sore?" He dug his thumbs into Trey's traps.

Trey cried out, melting against the tile.

"That's it, baby. God, that had to be a hellish drive." He rubbed harder, pushing deep.

"It was. I was trying to be calm for the boys, but damn."

"You did a good job. Cole was proud, and Braden was calm." Braden's words came back to him. *Uncle Daddy is old, way older than you.* "You're the backbone of this family."

"Someone has to be the boring one."

"You're not boring to me, baby." This was a theme, and he was beginning to get a weird feeling about it. Trey wasn't old or boring or dull.

"Thanks."

"No, I mean it. You keep acting like you're a thousand years old, and you're not thirty."

"I feel like an old man." Trey wouldn't look back at him, but to his credit, Ap was rubbing pretty hard.

"Well, you're not. You're a great dad, and you've kept this place together all along." Was that good? Maybe Trey wanted to hear how damn sexy he was.

"I—" Trey groaned. "Right there."

"Uh-huh." There was a spot on either side of that long spine that needed releasing.

"God. Ap. That makes me dizzy."

"You deserve to be made dizzy."

"I do?"

"Yes." Ap kissed the wet nape of Trey's neck. "You're sexy as hell, baby, and mine. I intend to keep you, you know."

"I'm not going anywhere, Ap. You don't have to keep me. I'll be here for you."

"Hey." Okay, that was the last straw. "We need to talk about some things, I think."

He could feel Trey begin to tense. "Sure, man. No problem."

"Shh. I'm not going anywhere, and no one did anything wrong, that I can tell. I just—we need it."

"What do you need to say, then?" Trey was trying not to be ugly, he could tell, and he appreciated it. Lord knew, they didn't have a lot of experience in talking. Hell, they both had been carrying a torch— Trey damn near religiously—and neither one had so much as said boo.

They had to do it. They had to say things, or they were going to fuck this up. That was what had happened years ago. They'd just been kids, but they should have talked over that huge span of time.

"You can't keep putting yourself down and thinking I just want to be with you when I'm off the road. It ain't true."

"I... I just let myself be all stupid, is all. It's been amazing, having you here—another adult, another person to work with, someone to make love to."

"So, why are you so mad?" That just burst out, not at all what he'd planned to say.

"Because you're waiting to leave. I'm having fantasies of being together, and you're already on the road. I'm a fool." Trey turned the water off, stepped out of the shower, and grabbed a towel.

He almost slipped and killed himself getting out after Trey. "What? I mean, last I looked, I was still right here?"

"I know, but it's like you said, you're ready to go." Trey wouldn't meet his eyes. "I don't blame you. You... you get to go and see. I'm so jealous. So proud too. Always."

"I'm not already on the road. I'm—is this because of what I said in the barn? Jesus, baby, I was just pissed off. I didn't mean it." Not to mention that he wasn't good enough to do anything else.

Trey sighed softly. "I was in the barn having fantasies. I... I want to work next to you, raise the babies, raise bulls. I'm tired of going it alone."

"Okay." He pulled Trey down on the bed to sit, despite them both being dripping wet. "What's wrong with that?" He wanted that too. So much. He wasn't sure what he could do to help keep them afloat, though.

"Nothing. Nothing. I think we could have a going thing. I'm doing good in the futurities, and with your contacts and experience, hell, your name, we could make something amazing."

Ap blinked. "You mean there's a use for me?" He chuckled. "Who knew?"

"You know bulls; you know the sponsors, the stock contractors—I… I'm real tired of working alone."

"I just… I never thought there was anything for me to do here, baby. I thought I could make better money on the road." He spread his hands. "Are we gonna be okay without that money?"

"I ain't used your money since the start, barring an emergency, and I've put it back in."

He shook his head. "Does that mean we're idiots?"

Trey snorted. "No, it means you've paid for five kids to go to college. For a new roof when we needed it. For that bucking bull so I didn't have to pay interest on a real loan, just pay back the emergency fund."

He searched Trey's face. "For real?"

"Yeah. For real. I just… I want you. Here. Home. Together with me and all." Trey's expression was about as honest as they came.

"That's what I want too. I can't promise I won't do local stuff…." He grinned when Trey took a swat. "I'm tired of sleeping in my truck."

"We can all come sometimes, cheer you on."

"I would love that." He sat there, feeling a little stunned. "Can we really do this?"

"I can." Trey finally, blessedly, looked at him, met his eyes, smiled. "I can do this with you, long-term."

"Then I'm in." He reached out to cup Trey's cheek with his palm. "No more putting yourself down. You're the core of this family, the strongest man I know. The best man I know. You gave up your whole life for Danny's babies. You… damn, baby. I love you."

That dark blush told him Trey had needed to hear that, had needed to hear him say it.

"I mean it, okay?" He wanted Trey to nod or say something to agree, just so he could see Trey knew he was serious.

"Thank you." Trey blinked a couple of times before just surging forward, kissing him hard.

He threw his arms around his cowboy and kissed back, feeling like he was in a movie or something. He'd never been so damn happy.

"Our room. Our bed. Ours." Trey covered him, threatening to squish him. "Our kids."

"Our house. My cowboy." He hugged Trey down to him. "I love you, baby."

"I love you. It's still snowing."

Yeah, it was still snowing, all their kids were snug abed, and they had all the food they could eat. "Sounds like a good Christmas Eve brewing."

"Mm-hmm. It does." Trey threw the heavy comforter over them, cocooning them. "If I get you off tonight, will you make me waffles in the morning?"

"I will make you anything you want." Ap chuckled. "Well, as long as we have it in the house. I'm not driving in this shit."

Chapter Twenty-Five

THE snow stopped about twilight Christmas Eve, and Cole and Ap went with Trey to do the nighttime feeding, make sure all the critters were snug. Those clouds were clearing, and it was going to be bitter by dawn.

The Christmas lights reflected off the snow, the smell of piñon sharp on the air. Lord, it was a New Mexico Christmas.

There was posole in the Crock-Pot, tamales and biscochitos on plates on the counter, where the dogs couldn't reach.

The girls were all curled up together, and Braden was wrapping the last-minute presents from the kids.

"You look all smug, Uncle Daddy." Cole sounded altogether too damn knowing for a kid who was sixteen.

"Do I? I'm happy, son."

"That's good, right? You need that."

"Yeah. Yeah. I do."

"What does that mean for us? I mean, us kids?"

"It means I'm staying home a lot more. That I'll ride the local circuit when I want to. That y'all better get used to having me around." Ap's words made his heart pound a little faster.

"Hey, I can handle it. Not so much driving!" Cole chortled. "Merry Christmas to me."

"Listen to you. Go feed those damn ostriches."

Ap groaned. "I want to discuss those huge evil dinosaur chickens, Cole."

Cole raised his eyebrows. "Yeah?"

"I think you should sell them."

Cole looked to Trey questioningly.

"That's up to you, son. They're yours. You might listen to what Ap has to say."

"They're eating feed and hurting people. What if one of them hurt Bella or something? I think I could help find a buyer who would get you enough money to buy new tires and more."

Trey hid his smile as Cole's eyes lit up. "Yeah? I could use tires, for real. Maybe get a calf too?"

"I bet." Ap grinned, looking tickled as a pig in shit. "So it's okay if I make some calls?"

"Yeah. Yeah. That would rock, thanks." Cole bounced in his boots.

"All right, let's get this done. I need coffee and posole."

"Me too." Ap was a little bouncy too. "And cookies. Amelia has been busy."

"She's really getting this cookie thing down." He was proud of her.

"Yeah, she—"

They all turned as the barn door opened. "I'm coming to help."

Bella.

Their cowgirl.

He looked to Ap. Ap looked at him, and they both turned to Bella, who was wearing her helmet.

"You can fill buckets, but no going in the stalls, kiddo," Ap said finally.

"Yes, sir." She smiled at Ap. "A cowboy takes care of her animals. Especially baby yaks."

"She's yours, Ap. To the bone."

"They all are. They're ours. Come on, y'all. It's friggin' cold out here."

They got the work done, because the ranch came first, but they didn't have to yell at Bella, so he would take it. They all hurried to get inside, because even the dogs wouldn't come out with them tonight.

They got in, finding Court and Amelia setting the table, Braden's phone playing Christmas carols as he made cocoa.

That was Christmas right there. His kids all there and safe, his lover with him. Ap was laughing, teasing the corgis and the lab who had appeared last week with a nonchocolate cookie.

Courtney came to him, arms up and open. He grabbed her up. "Hey, baby girl. You happy?"

"Uh-huh. Santa Claus comes tonight."

"He does."

"You look happy too. Did you know Cole got mistletoe?"

"Did he now?"

"Uh-huh. He kissed his girlfriend."

"Where did he hide it?"

"He didn't. He hanged it there." She pointed to the doorway to the laundry room.

Trey leaned in, whispering in her ear. "Do me a favor, baby girl?"

She nodded, so eager to help.

"Go get your Uncle Ap and bring him to the laundry room?"

Her pretty eyes went wide. "Are you going to kiss him?"

"I am."

"Wow. Okay!" She hopped out of his arms, made a beeline for Ap.

Trey moved to stand under the mistletoe while Court yanked at Ap's hand. "Uncle Daddy needs you!"

"Yeah? Is he okay?" Ap was smiling at Courtney, not looking toward him yet.

"Yes! He wants to kiss you!"

All eyes moved to Trey, the doorway, the mistletoe.

He forced himself not to shy away. Start out like you can hold out. The kids needed to see this, to know it was normal.

Ap laughed. "Well, now you're talking." He stormed over to twirl Trey into his arms, taking a dramatic kiss.

"Ew!" Braden and Bella both started gagging, while Cole got the little ones settled at the table for their Christmas Eve supper.

"Merry Christmas, Ap."

"Merry Christmas, baby." Ap kissed him one more time. "I can't wait for our happy New Year."

"For all the happy New Years to come. We've got a lot of babies to raise."

"Hey, I've got your back." Ap was going to be a handful if the way he goosed Trey was any indication.

Good thing he was an expert at handling everything that went on around here, from babies to yaks to those crazy rodeo cowboys.

Coming in October 2018

ⓓREAMSPUN DESIRES

Dreamspun Desires #67
The Spy's Love Song by Kim Fielding

For a singer and a spy, love might be mission impossible.

Jaxon Powers has what most only dream of. Fame. Fortune. Gold records and Grammy awards. Lavish hotel suites and an endless parade of eager bedmates. He's adored all over the world—even in the remote, repressive country of Vasnytsia, where the tyrannical dictator is a big fan. The State Department hopes a performance might improve US relations with a dangerous enemy. But it means Jaxon's going in alone… with one exception.

Secret agent Reid Stanfill has a covert agenda with global ramifications. Duty means everything to him, even when it involves protecting a jaded rock star. Jaxon and Reid's mutual attraction is dangerous under Vasnytsia's harsh laws—and matters get even worse when they're trapped inside the borders. Romance will have to wait… assuming they make it out alive.

Dreamspun Desires #68
Handle With Care by Cari Z.

A fragile heart needs extra care.

Burned-out social worker Aaron McCoy is on vacation for the first time in years—boss's orders. Road-tripping to his brother's wedding with his best friend, Tyler, seems a fun way to spend the mandatory two-week leave, and they set out for Kansas—and a difficult homecoming.

Aaron's mother was a drug addict, and his adorable younger brother was quickly adopted, while Aaron spent his childhood in foster care. As Aaron mends fences, Tyler hopes to show him that this time, he won't be left behind to face his problems alone.

Aaron's opening up to how right it feels to be with Tyler and to the possibility of taking the leap from friends to lovers. But along with the wedding celebration comes a painful reminder of the past. Aaron's heart is still breakable. Can he put it in Tyler's hands?